1

Evie drummed the steering wheel impatiently. She was going to be late. There was no-one to blame but herself — she should have allowed enough time to negotiate the twisting country roads that weaved their way towards the remote Scottish town of Balloch Pass. She'd almost reached her destination, but now she was caught in a traffic jam, of all things. Having hardly passed a car for twenty minutes previously, it was a surprise to suddenly grind to a halt. There were signs indicating a railway track up ahead; and, although she couldn't see the line from where she'd stopped, stuck behind a large transit van in the queue, the crossing must have shut for a train to pass.

She really didn't want to be late. Meeting with Alasdair James was enough to contend with as it was. She hadn't had the chance to speak to her new boss on the phone, let alone meet him in person. So she had no idea if he'd turn out to be the friendly, benevolent country doctor she pictured in her more positive moments . . . or the dour, curmudgeonly presence she envisaged when she woke up in the dead of night, in a cold sweat about what she'd done. Even in those moments, she couldn't regret her decision to take a job as far away from her old home as possible. She'd contemplated Alaska, and even the Australian Outback, but there would have been so much more to sort out — visas and work permits and so on. This was quick, and no-one would ever find her here, unless she wanted them to.

A huge crash made Evie jump, like the sound of a wrecking ball hitting the side of a building. It was followed by a scream that pierced the air and an unearthly wail. The man in the transit van in front jumped down onto the tarmac, turning briefly in her direction, terror etched on his face, before

FALLING FOR DR. RIGHT

In the wake of her mother's death and a broken engagement, Dr. Evie Daniels decides to travel the world, doing everything her mum never had the chance to. Leaving her London job, she accepts a temporary locum position in the remote Scottish town of Balloch Pass, where she finds herself enjoying the work and community — and her handsome colleague Dr. Alasdair James. The feeling is mutual — but Alasdair is bound to Balloch Pass, whilst Evie is committed to spreading her wings . . .

Books by Jo Bartlett
in the Linford Romance Library:

NO TIME FOR SECOND BEST
CHRISTMAS IN THE BAY

JO BARTLETT

FALLING FOR DR. RIGHT

Complete and Unabridged

LINFORD
Leicester

First published in Great Britain in 2016

First Linford Edition
published 2017

Copyright © 2016 by Jo Bartlett

A catalogue record for this book is available
from the British Library.

ISBN 978–1–4448–3327–0

Published by
F. A. Thorpe (Publishing)
Anstey, Leicestershire

Set by Words & Graphics Ltd.
Anstey, Leicestershire
Printed and bound in Great Britain by
T. J. International Ltd., Padstow, Cornwall

This book is printed on acid-free paper

hurtling towards the level crossing. There was shouting and another scream as Evie threw her car door open. Whatever it was, she had to see if she could help, her medical training kicking in and overriding any fear of what she might find.

She was several cars back from the crossing, but as soon as she passed the transit van she saw it: a car had overshot the barrier on the other side and ploughed through the wooden gates, splintering them like matchsticks. A woman standing just inside the barrier on the near side of the tracks was screaming hysterically, and at first Evie couldn't make out what she was saying. When she finally understood, she almost wished she hadn't.

'My baby's in the car. Please some-one, help me!' The woman screamed again, then seemed to just crumple towards the ground before Evie could even get close.

★   ★   ★

Dr. Alasdair James was only too aware that he had a duty to the people of Balloch Pass, and those in the surrounding countryside that spanned the boundaries of his practice, but fulfilling that duty was more of a burden with some patients than others. He'd been tempted to tell Angus McTavish that, no, there was absolutely no chance of him getting out to his farmstead this afternoon for a home visit, despite the elderly farmer insisting it was an emergency. After all, he was supposed to be meeting his new locum, Evie Daniels, at the Balloch Pass Inn in less than half an hour, and in all likelihood Angus just needed a bit of reassurance. There was always a chance, though, that for once the old man was telling the truth and he really did need medical attention.

Not able to risk it, despite the likelihood of the home visit being a waste of time, he'd left a message at the pub in case Dr. Daniels arrived before he got back. Now it seemed that the

4

call-out had been an act of fate, putting Alasdair in the right place at the right time — or the wrong place at the wrong time, depending on how you looked at it. Either way, this was a genuine emergency. There was a car up ahead on the tracks, and lots of shouting. Yanking the handbrake up, he stopped his car at the side of the road and raced towards the stranded vehicle, praying there was no-one inside.

'There's a bairn in the car, Doc, and her mother's just this second passed out.' Aggie Green, who ran the post office, was standing to one side of the smashed barrier, her face flushed with shock. 'I was just going to cross the tracks to collect a parcel from Father Douglas. You probably know he's hurt his foot and can't get out . . . ' She was babbling, and Alasdair gave a brief nod in her direction; now wasn't the time for niceties.

'Get the mother off the tracks to safety, and I'll take a look at her afterwards!' he shouted at two men standing just on the other side of the barrier on the far side of the tracks, who seemed to have frozen in panic at the sight that greeted them. He briefly noticed a slim, blonde woman sprinting towards them. He didn't recognise her, so she almost certainly wasn't local. Hopefully she'd have the sense to stay with the patient, when the men had moved her, and check she was breathing. There was no time to give any more instructions, though. They had to get the child out at the very least, plus move the car before the train came if they could; but right now, whoever was strapped into the back seat was his priority.

The car was straddling the middle of the crossing. The back door nearest to Alasdair had been stoved in by the force of it hitting the wooden barrier. He wrenched it as hard as he could, but it wouldn't budge. All the while, he kept his eyes fixed on the baby, who looked less than a year old, still strapped into his car seat and sobbing loudly. That was a good sign; he'd have been more worried if the child had been quiet.

Now they just needed to get him out.

'If the door won't move, shall we shift the car instead, Dr. James?' Alasdair looked up briefly as one of the men he'd instructed to move the woman to safety joined him on the crossing. Glancing round to check they'd followed his instructions, he shook his head and thrust his car keys towards the man who'd addressed him, who he recognised as one of his patients.

'There's a rope in the boot of my car. Attach it to the back bumper if you can, and pull it from the safety of the road on that side. I can't risk the two of you being on the tracks as well if the train comes. I'll get around the other side and climb in the driver's door to get the boy out. His mother got out that way, so I should be able to get in.'

★   ★   ★

Evie could tell, without having to move closer to the woman's face, that she was breathing. After the two men had

7

dragged her to safety, following instructions from another man who seemed to have taken charge of the situation, they'd left her to it. They were obviously going to try to move the car, but she couldn't think about that, or the fact that there was apparently a baby still trapped inside it. She needed to concentrate on the patient in front of her; she'd have to be kept calm when she came round, or she could hamper the attempts to rescue her child.

Evie checked her airway. There was no sign of any obvious injury from when she'd collapsed, but her pulse was rapid, so it was almost certainly shock and the sheer terror of the situation that had caused the collapse. Her own blood whooshed in her ears as she looked up at the two men on the other side of the crossing, still struggling to move the car. The third man was just visible leaning over the back of the driver's seat. *Please let him get the baby out okay.*

She wished she knew the woman's

name as she spoke to her in soft tones, reassuring her that everything was going to be okay. It was a pretty big stretch of the truth the way things stood.

Evie's head shot up as a train horn blasted. She'd never felt so powerless in her life — well, maybe once — and could hardly bear to watch as the noise of the approaching train grew ever more apparent. Suddenly, the man who'd been trying to rescue the child emerged from the vehicle. His back was to her for a second or two, so she couldn't see at first if he'd managed it. Then, as he turned to run over to the far side of the crossing, she caught sight of the baby cradled against his chest. The car had moved back slightly, but it wasn't completely clear of the tracks. Evie knew she should probably move; she was still too close if anything happened and the train derailed. She couldn't leave her patient, though, so she just watched as the freight train hurtled closer, finally ducking her head as its brakes screamed in vain.

* * *

'Everybody get back! Stop pulling the car and get out of the way!' Alasdair shouted the instruction as he cleared the tracks, the child cradled against his chest with one arm, grabbing Aggie Green by the wrist with his other hand as he ran past her. If the train hit the car, anything could happen. The men pulling it could be dragged with it, and Aggie, in her position by the gates, might be hit too. There was an almost-deafening squeal of brakes and the sound of metal crunching against metal before it all suddenly went quiet. Sitting Aggie down on the bank, Alasdair put the baby in her arms and turned back towards the railway line.

The train seemed to have pushed the car clear of the tracks — and, thank goodness, it hadn't derailed. It was a short freight train, but there was a good chance the driver had sustained an injury, so Alasdair ran up the side of the track towards the front of the train, the smell of burning from the emergency stop filling the air.

'Was there anyone in the car?' a man with a broad London accent addressed Alasdair as he drew level with the driver's window.

'No, they all got out.' He took in the driver's appearance. His face seemed to have drained of all colour, and Alasdair could hear how rapid his breathing was, even from his position on the side of the tracks.

'Oh, thank goodness!'

'What about you? Are you injured? Have you got any pain in your neck or back? That was a pretty rapid stop.'

'I'm f-f-fine. I braced myself for the stop.' The man's stuttering speech belied his words.

'Even if you haven't got a physical injury, it must have been a huge shock to see the car on the tracks. I'd like to have a look at you, I'm a doctor. My name's Alasdair, by the way. What's yours?'

'Ritchie.' The man shook his head.

'But I'm okay, really. See, I've been through all this before; just never thought I'd have it up here. I had two jumpers when I was driving trains in and out of London — both in less than two years. It nearly finished me, but I moved up this way, started driving freight on the rural lines . . . I just never imagined I'd get that terrible feeling again.'

'I really think you should let me have a look at you, Ritchie.' As Alasdair spoke, one of the men who'd helped get the car part way off the tracks came up behind him.

'The air ambulance is on the way apparently, Doc, plus the police and the fire brigade, so Aggie says. She called the emergency services as soon as she saw the accident, but she couldn't remember if she'd told you. I think we're all a bit shocked.' He shrugged, as though it was nothing really. 'Trust that lot to turn up when we've done it all! They've closed the line too, so at least we know there won't be another train speeding along any minute.'

'Thanks.' Alasdair had too many patients to know them all by name, but he had a good memory for faces, and the man was definitely one of his. It didn't matter now, though; they just needed to get the driver where he could be properly checked out. 'Will you help me get Ritchie down from the cab? Then we can get back to the others. I'd like to take a look at the boy's mother, just to make sure it isn't more than shock and she didn't injure herself when she collapsed.'

Between the two of them, they managed to help Ritchie down from the train. It was incredible how high up it was when you didn't have a station platform to give you an advantage. When Ritchie finally made it down to solid ground, his legs seemed to give way beneath him. Despite all his protests, the incident had obviously shocked him more than he wanted to let on, and Alasdair was keen to get him back to the safety of the side of the crossing so that he could take a good look at him. With the other man's help, they supported Ritchie to walk along the edge of the line.

As they reached the end of the train, the level crossing was visible up ahead, and the blonde woman who he'd noticed earlier looked like she was taking the pulse of the patient who'd collapsed. Someone had found a fold-up garden chair and the woman was sitting on it, her son on her lap, with Aggie Green jabbering away at the side of her. The blonde woman looked up as he got closer; it was completely inappropriate to notice how beautiful she was, but he did so all the same. She had high cheekbones, and the sort of spark in her sky-blue eyes he would have expected from someone who'd so readily taken charge of a difficult situation. She should have waited to move the woman again, though — for all she knew, she might have a head injury or damaged her spine. It was bad enough that they'd had to move her to safety once, but moving her again was completely unnecessary. Spark or not, there were some things that should be left to the professionals.

*   *   *

Evie had the advantage. The woman standing next to her, who seemed to cram far more syllables into a sentence than ought to be possible, had told her it was Dr. James who'd rescued the baby — now sitting happily on his mother's lap — from the stranded car, seconds before the freight train had rammed it off the track. The boy's mother was recovering well. She was still in shock, muttering about how she'd never be able to thank the doctor for saving her baby, when he suddenly hove into view. He was supporting a man who Evie could only assume was the train driver; and, once he'd checked him over and settled him down into the passenger seat of a car parked on the other side of the crossing, he turned and began striding in her direction.

Alasdair James was a poster boy for heroism: tall and broad-shouldered, with dark eyes that seemed to bore into hers as their gaze met. Her stomach did a funny little skip in response, but it was just nerves. Here she was, about to speak to her impossibly good-looking new boss for the first time, and he didn't look like he was going to relish the meeting. She only hoped it was because he didn't know who she was — rather than that he did, but didn't like what he saw.

'Who moved this woman again?' Dr. James looked straight at her and it was clear he already knew the answer. His full lips were set in a firm line, a muscle going in his cheek. It looked like she might be out of a job before she'd even started.

'I did, I . . . '

'She could have a head injury or spinal damage after that fall. The more you move her, the more chance there is of something like that doing irreparable damage.' He cut her off before she could get the words out, but the look on his face softened as he spoke and her stomach did another little skip in response. Damn. This was not what she'd had in mind when she'd decided to leave London. This was supposed to be about an uncomplicated rural life, but there was nothing uncomplicated about the reaction her body had, all by itself, every time Alasdair looked in her direction. 'Look, I know you were only trying to help, but you can cause real problems when you don't know what you're doing. You should have left it to a professional.'

'I spoke to the patient before I moved her.' Evie glanced down at the woman in the chair, who was staring wide-eyed at Alasdair, her mouth hanging half open — no wonder he thought she might have sustained a head injury. Evie suspected he had this effect on women a lot of the time, but he seemed blissfully unaware of both his good looks and his status as hero of the

17

moment. Alarmingly, that made him all the more attractive. 'I did a neck-and-back assessment, and she was zero grade. No complaints of pain, and no physical symptoms to suggest she'd injured her spine in any way. She was perfectly coherent when I carried out the Glasgow Coma Scale, too. She could answer all my questions and had no issues moving her eyes or limbs. She seems to have had a lucky escape, despite her airbag not deploying and the subsequent fall. Of course, I'd recommend she goes to the hospital when the paramedics arrive, just for both of them to be checked over, but I felt confident to move her.' Evie forced herself to look at Alasdair levelly, aware that she sounded defensive but hoping he would at least recognise her professionalism.

'Dr. Evie Daniels, I presume?' Alasdair's serious expression was replaced by a smile, as he held out his hand towards her. 'Quite a baptism of fire we've given you this afternoon. I'm Alasdair James by the way.'

'Yes, it was quite a welcome.' She took his proffered hand, the same warmth there as was evident in his voice. He definitely wasn't the dour, ancient GP she'd feared. 'And there I was thinking life up here would be quiet after working in London.'

'That's exactly what the train driver said.' Alasdair smiled again and it was like a weight had been lifted from Evie's shoulders. She was going to like working with him, she was sure of it. 'I'd better go and wait with him actually, now I know you've got everything in hand with these two.' He gestured towards the baby on his mother's lap, who looked like nothing of any significance had happened to him.

'Of course.' Evie returned his smile as the boy's mother continued to stare at Alasdair, apparently still unable to find the words to express her gratitude. 'I'll stay with them until the ambulance gets here, and then perhaps we can meet up a bit later than originally planned?'

19

'Absolutely. After all this is sorted out, I've got to go up to a farm about a mile out of town to see a patient. So shall we say seven o'clock, to be on the safe side?' Evie nodded in response and Alasdair reached out, brushing his hand against her forearm with the briefest of touches. 'I can't promise it's always going to be this exciting, but welcome to Balloch Pass, Dr. Daniels. I've got a feeling you're just what this town's been waiting for.'

'Thank you. I hope so.' Evie breathed out slowly as Alasdair turned and crossed the railway, opening the car door to speak to the train driver again. Balloch Pass had already thrown up its fair share of surprises, and she suddenly had an overwhelming urge to phone someone back home and tell them what had happened. Only there was no-one left to call.

2

Lying to yourself was a waste of time, but Evie was doing it all the same. She wasn't applying her make-up with extra care because Dr. Alasdair James looked as though he'd just stepped out of an aftershave advert, with that barest hint of a Scottish accent that was far sexier than she'd ever imagined it would be. No, she was doing this for herself, to create a good impression with the locals — half of whom, judging from the raucous laughter that drifted up from the bar every few minutes, were regulars of the Balloch Pass Inn. The landlady had warned her she had a hard act to follow at the surgery when she'd checked in, having booked a room above the Inn for her first couple of weeks in town. If it was meant as a welcome greeting, it hadn't done much to calm her nerves. So she needed all the help she could in get in creating a good impression.

Five to seven. It wouldn't do much for that good impression to be late, but she wasn't particularly keen on the idea of hanging around in the bar by herself, either. She could nurse a drink for five or ten minutes, though. It wasn't like it was the first time she'd been kept waiting by a man . . . but things were different in London. You could sit in a bar there — probably for days, as long as you kept paying for drinks — without anyone asking if you were okay. Balloch Pass, on the other hand, was a whole other world.

Descending the stairs to the pub, which were flanked with dark wood panelling, the sight of Alasdair already leaning against the bar was a welcome one.

'Sorry. I'm not late, am I?' Evie twisted the bracelet round her wrist. He had an unnerving way of looking at her, as if he could see beyond the outer façade she'd worked so hard to create these last few months.

'Not at all. Can I get you a drink?' He'd barely leant an inch or two across the bar before the young barmaid instantly appeared, like a genie emerging from a bottle.

'What can I get you, Doc, the usual?' She shot Evie a look as she spoke, which wasn't altogether friendly.

'Yes please, Lyndsay — and what can I get you, Evie?'

'I'll have a white wine spritzer, please.' Evie didn't often drink, especially on a weeknight, but nerves were getting the better of her now that she was actually here and the locals didn't appear entirely welcoming. It needn't be for long, though. She repeated the mantra in her head as she took a seat at a table to the left of the bar and waited for Alasdair next to a big open fireplace that was unlit at this time of year. *No long-term commitments until she was sure.* Balloch Pass was just a step on the road.

'I'm sorry about earlier.' Alasdair set the drink down on the table in front of his new locum. No wonder Lyndsay had been so hostile: it was a long time since she'd had this sort of competition in town. If they'd had such a thing as Homecoming Queen, the Balloch Pass Inn's barmaid would definitely have volunteered for the job, but she wasn't even in Dr. Daniel's league. Waves of dark blonde hair framed Evie's face, and when she directed those big blue eyes towards him, it was hard not to ask her questions of a much more personal nature than their new working relationship warranted. 'You handled that incident on the crossing brilliantly, but it wasn't exactly the introduction to life here I wanted you to have.'

'It wasn't something that could really be planned for!' She laughed, those killer blue eyes creasing in the corners. 'Anyway, what I did was nothing compared with you saving the baby. I've been wondering ever since how on earth his mother ended up on the tracks. She was too traumatised to make much sense of it when I was with her.'

'Apparently she just lost control of the car and put her foot on the wrong pedal. At least, that's what she told the police.' Alasdair took a sip of his beer, remembering the look of terror on the young mother's face as she'd recounted the events leading up to her overshooting the barrier, once the police had arrived and Evie had headed off. 'It doesn't bear thinking about what might have happened if we hadn't been there.' Memories of another car accident he could do absolutely nothing about clouded his thoughts. A repeat of that outcome *really* didn't bear thinking about.

'Oh I think you could have managed without me. You, on the other hand; that's a different matter.' She looked straight at him as she spoke, and as he held her gaze, her cheeks seemed to colour. It was hot in the pub, though, and another crowd of locals had just come in, standing two-deep at the bar in front of them. It seemed everyone wanted to check out the new locum, and he hadn't missed the way some of the men looked at her, although he could hardly blame them.

'Don't sell yourself short,' Alasdair said, breaking the tension. 'So, how long do you think you'll stay with us? The agency tell me you aren't interested in a permanent post.'

'I didn't think there *was* one.' Nerves seemed to be getting to her, but he hadn't meant to put her on the spot.

'There isn't — at least, not for the moment.' Peter Tennant, his partner in the practice, was never too far from his thoughts, and his good mood at having found such an able locum began to slip away. *Beauty, brains and bravery* — Evie Daniels seemed to have it all, but she'd still never come close to replacing his closest friend. Pete had left an unfillable void.

'In that case, I think perhaps we're made for each other.' Evie caught his eye as she spoke. She was definitely blushing this time.

'Well, that is good news.' He couldn't resist teasing her, even though he probably shouldn't.

'I just meant that *you* don't need a doctor at the surgery long-term, and *I'm* not planning on settling down any time soon.' She blushed again, this time a deeper shade of pink. 'That's coming out all wrong. I just meant I . . . '

'I know what you meant.' He laughed at the expression on her face. 'This is the twenty-first century, after all. The last thing I'd assume is that you were on some mission to find a husband.'

'And you'd be dead right. Young, free, single, and on the road — that's me from now on.' There was something behind her eyes, something that suggested there was a lot more to her story than she was willing to tell him right now. That was okay, though — she was just passing through, and he didn't need to know the ins and outs of her past or her future. He'd been down that road before. There was nothing he didn't know about Peter, and now it seemed Alasdair's own future was all mapped out for him as a result — whether he was ready for it or not.

★ ★ ★

'I've ordered the food.' Alasdair returned to the table, and Evie was forced to stop going over the things she'd said to him. She seemed to develop a bad case of foot-in-mouth syndrome whenever he looked at her. At almost thirty years old, she was an experienced medical professional who'd seen more high drama in her professional and personal life than she wanted to think about. So why was she reduced to an incoherent bag of nerves when Alasdair shot her one of his intense looks? Why one earth had she said they were *made for each other*, or mentioned *settling down*? He might have said he didn't think she was looking for

Mr. Right, but she'd sure as heck given him every reason to suppose otherwise. It wasn't her fault, though, it was his eyes . . . and his lips. She found herself staring at them whenever he was talking, and not thinking before she spoke as a result. She'd better get over it quickly, find something else to focus on, or he'd be contacting the agency to ask for someone else before she knew it.

'Thank you. I hadn't realised how hungry I was.' Despite stopping at a couple of service stations on route from her overnight stop in Manchester, it had still been an incredibly early start and a long day. Maybe that was the real reason she couldn't seem to string two words together.

'So why this post in Balloch Pass? I gather you were based in London before?' He fixed her with his inquisitive brown eyes, in the sort of look he must use on patients when he wanted to know if they were really sticking to their healthy eating plan.

'Yes, it's a long way from home.'

Home. It was such an emotive word that held so many promises of what would be waiting there. Only all those things had gone now, and the concept of home had gone with them. 'I think that's the point, really. I decided it was time to travel a bit. Starting with the other end of the UK, and then — who knows? I think it will probably be somewhere overseas next.'

'It's something I thought about doing myself, but somehow the years went by, I ended up in partnership in the practice, and here I am: a fixture of Balloch Pass, for better or worse.' He looked suddenly wistful. 'You should do all that whilst you're still free to do so.'

Evie didn't know why she was surprised. Of course he was married; why wouldn't he be? The mention of being here *for better or worse* confirmed it. He wasn't wearing a ring, though. Not that she'd specifically checked, it was just one of those things you couldn't help noticing — on some people, at least.

'So, does your wife work in Balloch Pass too?' She wondered briefly if Mrs. James minded her husband having dinner with his new locum. Still, not all men were like her ex. Maybe Alasdair could be trusted. She wanted to believe he could, that *someone* could.

'My wife?' Alasdair laughed, his hypnotically full lips curving up in the corners as he did. 'You obviously haven't had a thorough briefing from Maggie yet!' He indicated the landlady, who was now standing behind the bar and staring openly in their direction. 'She despairs of my bachelor status, and I'm sure you'll hear about it at length.'

'So, what's stopping you going off on your own adventure, then? It wouldn't have to be forever, lots of my colleagues in London took sabbaticals to do it. What about a year with Médicins Sans Frontières? After your heroics on the railway line, I'm sure you'd fit in well.' The expression on his face changed as she spoke, some of the openness disappearing from it. 'Sorry, it's really none of my business.'

'It's fine. I just made a commitment to the practice and the people here.' He smiled, but it didn't quite reach his eyes. 'So I'm around for the long haul.'

By the time they'd eaten their meals — huge plates of fish and chips that could have fed a small army — Alasdair had given her the lowdown on many of the processes at the surgery, everything from opening times to the specialist clinics they ran. None of it sounded too daunting, but each time she tried to find out more about the GP she was taking over from, Alasdair had closed down a little bit more. All he'd said was that they'd had a couple of long-term locums over the past year, and that he needed a bit more time to work out what type of candidate might be the right fit for the surgery in the longer term. Whatever it was he'd chosen not to tell her, and just why his previous partner in the practice was so hard to replace, were significant. She had a feeling she'd have a much better chance of fitting in at Balloch Pass when she knew the full story about her predecessor.

'Is there anything else you want to ask me before we start tomorrow?' Alasdair opened the small leather-bound folder containing their bill, having already dismissed her offer of paying half.

'No, I think that's everything I wanted to cover. Although I'm sure I'll have lots more questions for you tomorrow.' Now wasn't the time to press him for more information about the doctor she was replacing. Evie let go of the breath she hadn't realised she was holding. Being a locum might offer variety and travel, but it would also mean making a new start every time, trying to build relationships with new people, and that wasn't always easy when you wanted to keep some things to yourself too.

'I'm really looking forward to working with you.' Alasdair stood up as he spoke and she rose to shake his hand, relieved that he seemed to mean what he said, despite his unwillingness to talk about her predecessor.

'Thank you. I can't wait to get started.' It was true. Burying herself in work had been her salvation, and it was time to get back to it.

Watching Alasdair leave the pub was like seeing a rock star try to get off stage through the crowd; everyone seemed to want a word with him and there were lots of pats on the back — news about his daring rescue from the crossing seeming to have spread around town in no time.

'How was your meal, hen?' A voice interrupted her thoughts and Evie turned to see Maggie, the landlady, clearing their plates from the end of the table. She was in her late fifties, with the sort of deeply furrowed brow that suggested she spent a long time listening in to other people's conversations.

'Lovely, thanks. Too huge for me to

manage, but it really was delicious.'

'We're glad to have you here.' Maggie stopped wiping up for a moment and reached out to put a hand over Evie's. 'It's about time Doc James had someone to lean on — professionally and personally.'

Evie suppressed a smile. Alasdair hadn't been wrong about the landlady and her desire to seem him change his bachelor status. In any case, she didn't want to be subject of more gossip than she had to be, so maybe now was a good time to embellish the truth a bit. 'I'm really glad to be here too to help Dr. James in the practice; but as for the rest, I'm not sure my fiancé in London would be too thrilled.'

'A fiancé, you say?' Maggie's brow furrowed a bit deeper, and for a moment she looked wrong-footed, but then she shook her head. 'Aye, that's as maybe, hen, but I've a way of knowing these things and I'd still bet on the two of you ending up together, you'll see. I'm never wrong when it comes to matters of the heart.'

It was Evie's turn to shake her head. She was suddenly desperate to finish her drink and get back up to her room. Tomorrow, with the normality of everyday work in the surgery, couldn't come too soon. Even if her fiancé was already well and truly in the ex-zone, that didn't mean Maggie was right about the rest. Another relationship was almost the last thing she wanted — the only thing she wanted less was to finish her journey before it began and end up stuck in a town like this. As adamant as she had been, this time the landlady of the Balloch Pass Inn was definitely wrong.

3

Evie had more time on her hands than she'd expected on her first morning at the surgery. Alasdair had ensured her appointments were kept to a minimum so she'd have time to get to grips with the computer systems and familiarise herself with the equipment on offer in the consulting rooms and the clinic, which was staffed twice-weekly by a part-time practice nurse. It was all quite low-key after the last surgery she'd worked for in North London, which ran the whole suite of NHS services and additional private services on the side, including non-surgical facelifts and other cosmetic treatments. Not that that was an area of medicine Evie had ever personally wanted to branch into. Community practice had always had her heart, making a difference to people's lives, and sometimes even contributing to saving one or two. Sadly, personal experience had shown that sometimes there was *nothing* you could do.

'Is it always this quiet?' Evie went out to the waiting room and spoke to Susie, the receptionist, who was sorting through a pile of repeat prescription requests.

'No, it's usually packed in here — especially lately, since the last locum left and Dr. James has been running the place on his own.' Susie looked up and smiled. 'He's got a double appointment in at the moment, and his next patient hasn't turned up yet. Your first patient isn't due for another twenty minutes, as he wanted you to have the morning to settle in.'

'That was thoughtful of him.' Evie suppressed a sigh and straightened up the copies of *The People's Friend* and *Car Monthly*, which were on the table in the centre of a horseshoe-shaped arrangement of chairs, just waiting for patients to arrive. She'd really wanted to get stuck in, and twenty minutes could seem like a lifetime when you had nothing to do but wait. Still, she'd probably be complaining about her workload before too long. There were never enough hours in the day to spend as long with your patients as you wanted to, so she might as well make the most of it.

'I think I'll just go and check the clinic roster again, Susie, so I can make sure I'm referring patients to our services where they meet their needs.' The words were barely out of her mouth when the surgery door flew open. A teenage boy of about sixteen had another, much younger, boy in his arms.

'It's my brother, he's swallowed a plastic building brick and it's stuck in his throat. He can't breathe!' The older boy was almost white with shock, and one look at his younger brother told Evie all she needed to know. His face had gone dark red and his eyes were streaming.

'Get Alasdair, quickly please, Susie.' Evie's voice sounded much calmer than she felt. There was no time to wait, but she'd need Alasdair's help if she couldn't dislodge the brick herself. Looking down the little boy's throat, she could see the top part of a blue building block. There was no time to try and remove it manually. He'd still been thrashing around when his brother had brought him in, but suddenly he'd gone limp, and his face had taken on a blueish tinge as if all the fight had gone out of him.

'We need to turn him over.' She moved the boy into a position where she could hit him firmly on the back, between his shoulder blades. She repeated the process five times, but nothing happened.

'He'd dying, please, you've got to do something!' His older brother was on the verge of hysteria, pacing like a caged animal and throwing his arms up into the air.

'Okay, I'm going to try something else. If that doesn't work, we might need to make an incision into his throat so he can breathe.' Evie stood up with her hands just above the boy's waist, pulling inwards and upwards as hard as she could. There was always a chance she might break his ribs, given his age, but it was far better than the alternative. With the first two attempts, nothing happened, and she looked up to see Alasdair running towards her. Part of her wanted him to take over, but the other half knew that nothing in the world could make her give up on trying to help this little boy. She repeated the abdominal thrust again; they'd have no choice but to perform an emergency tracheotomy if it didn't work soon. Alasdair was less than four feet away from her when the building brick suddenly shot out of the boy's mouth, hitting the doctor squarely in the chest before it fell to his feet.

'Well done, Evie. Is his airway clear now?' Alasdair looked at her levelly, bringing her back down to earth. There was so much adrenaline pumping through her veins, it felt as though her feet were barely touching the floor.

'He's breathing, but I think we should get him on some oxygen anyway until the ambulance gets here.' Evie lifted up the child as she spoke and nodded at Susie, who was already picking up the phone. 'We're going to take him through to the clinic.'

'Are you okay, Jared?' Alasdair put an arm round the older boy, who slumped against him. 'Try and slow down your breathing a bit; it won't help Drew if you pass out, he needs you here to keep him calm.'

'You know the boys, then?' Evie turned to look at Alasdair, once they were in the treatment room and she'd lain the younger boy on the bed.

'They live a few houses down from here, and their mum cleans the surgery.' Alasdair helped Jared into a chair. 'Come on, breathe slowly now. Take a long breath in, and then slowly let it out.' The older boy's breathing was raspy and his hands were shaking.

'He's only six. Mum's going to kill

me. She's out on a job, cleaning some new-builds in Draimsdeen.' Jared seemed to be shivering as the shock really began to set in. 'Drew's got a cold, so he wanted to stay off school, I'm not at college on a Thursday, so I said I'd look out for him. She's going to kill me,' he repeated, looking as if it might be a relief to him if she did.

'It's alright, Jared. I'll talk to your mum for you. The important thing is that you and Drew are both okay.' Alasdair crouched down by the boy, his soft brogue finally appearing to soothe Jared. Evie could listen to that voice all day if she had the chance, but right now there were more important things to do.

'My throat hurts.' Drew opened his eyes and began clawing at his face as Evie tried to put the oxygen mask over his mouth. 'I want my mummy!'

'It's alright, sweetheart.' She stroked the little boy's hair. 'You had a nasty building block caught in your throat, and it's scratched it a bit, but you're going to be okay now.'

'Is he really going to be okay?' His brother was up and pacing again. 'You're not just saying that, are you?' Fear twisted Jared's face.

'He's regained consciousness and he's talking; they're both excellent signs.' Alasdair put a hand on Jared's shoulder as he spoke. He was gentle but firm, just the sort of person Evie would want around in her hour of need. Not that she ever wanted to lean on a man for support again. She'd tried that once and been badly let down.

'What happened?' Alasdair placed both his hands on the boy's shoulders, which had at least stopped him pacing for a moment.

'We were playing a game. A stupid game.' Jared looked down at his shoes as he spoke. 'We were seeing how many building blocks we could fit in our mouths at once. Drew said he could beat me, but I told him there was absolutely no way he could.'

'Not the most sensible thing you've ever done.' Alasdair was keeping his tone calm and Evie found herself wondering if anything threw him off-track. 'Just promise me you won't do it again?'

She might have been angrier if the boy hadn't already been so terrified, but Alasdair was doing the right thing taking the gentle approach in the circumstances. Jared had well and truly learned his lesson, she was sure of it.

'I'll never go near the things again. I think I swallowed a brick too, one of the long thin ones, when Drew started to choke. Will it just come out on its own?' The boy touched his throat. 'I think it might still be there, it feels stuck, like I've got a golf ball wedged in there.' Jared coughed hard and then took in a huge gulp of air. 'It's moved.' His voice was getting raspier and he was suddenly struggling to speak. Alasdair took hold of his shoulders again.

'There's nothing visible in the throat, but I think he might have got it lodged further down in the trachea.' Alasdair shook his head. 'Why the hell didn't you mention that when you first came in?'

'He was terrified.' Evie continued to stroke Drew's hair, as Alasdair attempted to dislodge the object by repeating the abdominal thrust she'd done only moments before on the little boy.

'What's going on?' Drew tried to sit up on the bed and remove his oxygen mask, as Evie moved to shield his view. The last thing he needed was to start panicking now.

'It's okay, sweetheart, Dr. James is just making Jared better too.' Turning towards Alasdair, she could tell he was worried, as he tried the abdominal thrust for a third time. 'What do you want me to do?'

'Can you take Drew back to your room and get Susie to sit with him? I don't think this is coming out and he's starting to go blue. Goodness knows what he's swallowed — there could be several bricks down there, or something lodged on an angle that's inflamed his throat. Either way, I think his trachea is swollen; we need to get his airway open.'

Evie knew what that meant. An emergency tracheotomy would keep the oxygen supplied to his body until they could somehow remove the object lodged in his throat. It was their only option, but definitely not something she wanted his little brother to witness.

'The ambulance is on its way.' Susie smiled as Evie burst out of the treatment room with Drew in her arms, the oxygen supply still attached, clearly under the misapprehension that every-thing was under control. Alasdair's patient, whose appointment had been suddenly cut short, sat with a magazine clenched in his hands which he wasn't even attempting to read.

'Can you sit with Drew in my room, please, until the ambulance gets here?' Evie was really struggling to keep her voice steady now. 'There's been a bit of an emergency.' *Involving his brother*, she mouthed, so as not to scare the little boy, and Susie nodded her head, running around from her side of the reception desk and taking the boy from Evie's arms. 'I've got to go in and help Alasdair, but I'll be back down to you as soon as I can.'

Turning back towards the treatment room, Evie offered up a prayer that Alasdair had managed to dislodge the brick, and made a silent promise never to complain about a quiet morning again.

'It's still stuck and he's stopped breathing, there's no sound at all.' Alasdair had put Jared on the bed that his little brother had only just vacated. 'Can you get his head into position?'

Evie nodded and grabbed a blanket, still in its packaging, from the top of the nurse's desk. Ripping off the cellophane, she rolled it up, positioning it under Jared's shoulders to make his neck more accessible as Alasdair threw open cupboard doors to locate a tracheotomy kit.

'Will you hold his head?' Alasdair prepared what he needed to carry out the procedure as he spoke.

'I'm ready.' Evie positioned herself with one hand on either side of the boy's head.

'Whatever you do, don't let him move.' Alasdair looked at her and their eyes met for a second. The skin on Jared's face was definitely tinged with blue, and Evie fought to keep her own breathing regular. If Alasdair was fazed, he didn't show it, his hand steady as he performed the procedure. Within seconds, the skin on Jared's face was already turning pink, his chest rising and falling in a regular rhythm.

'Oh thank goodness.' Evie breathed the words and looked up at Alasdair.

'I wasn't sure if it was going to work. There was no way of knowing what had got lodged in there or how far down it was, and we haven't got a ventilator on site.' For the first time, he betrayed some vulnerability, and it made her want to comfort him, the way she'd comforted Drew. He'd performed a minor miracle and saved a life — for the second day in a row. In fact, they both had. Not bad for a quiet morning's work. 'You were brilliant with his little brother, by the way.' Alasdair smiled — those lips of his were miracle workers too; they had the power to make her forget about everything else.

'I think we make a good team.' It was safer ground than saying they were the perfect match, and Evie wasn't about to make the same mistake twice, even if her legs felt as though they'd turned to jelly. She couldn't even be sure if that was entirely down to the emergency they'd just faced.

'I think we make a pretty good team, too.' Alasdair looked for a moment as if he might say something else and then a disjointed voice sounded from the reception area.

'Paramedics. Someone called us.'

'I'll go and fill them in, if you don't mind staying with Jared?' Alasdair turned to look at her again as he got to the door. 'I told the agency I wanted you on a week's trial in the first instance; but after this, I think I'll cancel that. You're more than welcome to stay as long as you like.'

* * *

The rest of the day passed in relative calm after the drama of the morning, and there was nothing Evie hadn't felt able to handle without consulting Alasdair. She'd gone for a walk in her lunch break, needing to clear her head. The beauty of the scenery wasn't lost on her, though. Walking past a field that seemed to roll like green velvet as far as the eye could see, she was greeted by the sight of a large Highland cow looking in her direction. At least, she thought it was looking at her: it was hard to tell since the poor thing had a bright orange fringe completely covering its eyes. At least she wasn't the only one having a bad hair day. A sensible up-do had seemed the best thing to create a good impression on her first day, but it was too formal, and so rigid with hairspray it could probably withstand the harshest of Highland weather — rather than a sunny day in early September — not to mention her performing the Heimlich manoeuvre several times over. Evie's mother had always told her she looked like her old headmistress with her hair up like that. She bit her lip at the thought. Would it ever get easier thinking about what her mum *would* have said?

The sound of a tractor backfiring in a neighbouring field sent the cow and the rest of its herd scattering across the field, and Evie had headed back to the practice, firmly pushing thoughts of her old life to the back of her mind — just as she always did.

By the end of the day, she felt as if she'd been in Balloch Pass for weeks. She'd been introduced to Mrs. MacDonald's varicose veins, heard all about Katy Wilson's thwarted attempts to fall pregnant, and learnt that her predecessor — Dr. Peter Tennant — had been held in just as high regard as Alasdair. The reason Alasdair hadn't wanted to talk about Peter became clear when Mrs. MacDonald told Evie about the tragic accident that had killed Peter and his wife, leaving their children in the care of their uncle. The older woman had tears in her eyes as she recounted the tale. It seemed that Balloch Pass had suffered more than its share of tragedy over the past year, and Alasdair's tendency to shut down conversations every now and then made a lot more sense.

'How was your first day?' Alasdair was waiting for her when she emerged from her consulting room after seeing the last patient.

'Oh, you know, run-of-the-mill: choking incidents twice over and an emergency tracheotomy.' She smiled. 'Same old, same old.'

'You seem to have a knack for attracting medical emergencies.'

'It keeps us in work! Anyway, you were the one who told me you couldn't promise it would always be exciting. I think you sold Balloch Pass short.'

'Aye, I did, but I hadn't reckoned on the excitement you'd bring to town.' He retuned her smile, and she tried not to overanalyse his words, deciding to just take it as a compliment — it was far easier that way.

'How are the boys, by the way? Any news?'

'It turns out Jared had a long building brick wedged diagonally in his throat — it must have made things worse when he tried to cough it up. His trachea was swollen and closing up in response to the trauma, which was why his reaction was so delayed compared with Drew's. They're both doing well now, although their mother told me they'll be grounded for life once they're fully recovered.' Alasdair grinned. 'Still, boys will be boys, and they'll always get up to daft antics when they're left to their own devices.'

'Girls can get up to antics, too.' There she was, doing it again, inadvertently flirting with the best-looking man who'd crossed her path for a very long time, maybe even ever. It seemed beyond her control: her brain was saying one thing, and her mouth something else altogether.

'I'd like to have taken you out for a drink tonight, to talk over your first day, but I've got somewhere else I need to be.' Alasdair looked at his watch but, if his expression was anything to go by, he was genuinely disappointed. 'Although I hear you have a fiancé back in London who might not take too kindly to us socialising outside of work, anyway?'

'That's, er, he's not . . . ' Darn. The jungle drums didn't hang about in Balloch Pass. Her landlady must have been spreading that particular gem before Evie had even left the bar last night.

'Look, it's none of my business if you have or you haven't. It's just worth bearing in mind that anything you say in front of Maggie Hendry will be taken down and used in her next gossip bulletin.' Alasdair shrugged. 'That's just life in Balloch Pass; but don't let it get to you. I meant what I said earlier, you've been fantastic today, and I hope you'll stick around for a bit. I really do.'

She watched Alasdair head out to his car as their receptionist began the process of locking up. His wheels span slightly on the gravel when he reversed, sending a small shower of stones up into the air behind him. Wherever it was he was headed, he was in a hurry. Probably to meet a woman: the thought grated on Evie far more than she wanted to admit.

* * *

Alasdair pulled up outside the familiar house that had once been the scene of so much joy. He wasn't looking forward to this visit, and the thought of sharing a drink with Evie had almost melted his resolve. He didn't believe that story about a fiancé in London. He could tell by her face it wasn't true. Not that he blamed Evie for feeding her landlady that line; it was none of anyone's business what went on in her personal life. But that didn't stop him being pleased when her reaction convinced him the fiancé was a work of fiction — he was only human, after all.

Despite Evie being on his mind, it wasn't the thought of missing out on a drink with her that was making him dread going inside. Even after more than a year, being inside his best friend's home, without him in it, was difficult. It seemed so empty without Pete and Isabella there, even though Pete's brother Josh did his best to keep things as close to how they had been for the children. Hard as he tried, Josh was the first to admit he wasn't really cut out for taking on the role of mum and dad, and Alasdair knew that giving up his career in marine biology after his their deaths had been a huge wrench for Josh. Now it looked as if it might be a sacrifice he couldn't make after all, and it was another reason Alasdair was so reluctant to go inside.

Pete and Isabella has been one of those couples who seemed to have it all, and his old friend has changed almost beyond recognition when he'd met her. She'd even managed to get him to join in on their infamous games nights — him, a man who'd once walked five miles home in the snow rather than join in with some karaoke! When they'd married, all that had changed. Alasdair had envied their love: he'd never had anything close to the all-consuming feeling Peter had described to him on the eve of the wedding. So it seemed almost inevitable that they'd be together when they were taken so suddenly and cruelly on a treacherous piece of road known locally as 'the leather bootlace'. Isabella had been driving, and the police said she'd lost control of the car on a patch of oil which had seeped across one of the many hairpin bends in the road. Thank heavens the children had been at their weekend swimming lessons at the time — but they were left without either parent, and Alasdair couldn't do anything to put that right. It had made him realise his limitations as a doctor; there'd been nothing he could do except fulfil the promise he'd made to Peter and Isabella and take his role as godfather seriously.

The instructions in their will had been for Alasdair and Josh to share custody, with a request that the children be brought up in the home where they'd always lived. Just after his daughter was born, Pete had asked if Alasdair would be willing to take on the role of guardian in the unlikely event that anything should happen to both him and Isabella. All her family were in Italy, and Peter and Josh's parents had both passed on, so Alasdair had willingly agreed. It had seemed so unlikely back then that anything would happen to *either* of them, let alone both of them.

After the funeral, Josh had moved in to take care of the children, and Alasdair had offered all the support he could. He and Josh talked through decisions together, and the kids had been amazingly resilient as only children could be. He'd become friends with Josh, too, over the sixteen months since the accident, and it had been of comfort to him to have Peter's brother around. He wanted to tell Josh about Evie, to sing her praises, tell him how brilliant she'd been, but the last thing he wanted was for Josh to think his brother was easily replaced. There was no-one out there who could fill the hole he and Isabella had left behind, and now that Josh was thinking about moving on, he wasn't sure he could even attempt it on his own.

'Josh, it's me.' Alasdair let himself in with the key he'd been given so that he could come and go as he liked. Josh had laughed when Alasdair suggested he should knock 'just in case', and had told him that his personal life, like his career, had gone completely off the boil since he'd started taking care of his nephew and niece. Little Bronte was only five, her brother Rory eight, but more like a forty-year-old man trapped in a little boy's body. He'd had to grow up far too fast, something it hurt Alasdair to witness.

'Ali! I've been waiting all day to hear about the new locum,' Josh greeted him as he walked into the lounge, looking up from his laptop as he did.

'She's okay.' Alasdair smiled at the look on Josh's face.

'That's not the report I had back from the lads who were in the pub last night!'

'So, they made an appraisal of Evie's medical abilities, did they?' Alasdair clearly hadn't been wrong about the impact she'd had.

'Give me a break, mate, I haven't been on a date in almost eighteen months, and a guy's got to have a little bit of vicarious excitement.' Josh grinned. 'But there's absolutely nothing stopping *you*, Dr. James.'

'There might be. If you decide to take the job . . . ' Alasdair clenched his jaw. It was a difficult conversation to have, and the two of them had edged around it ever since Josh had mentioned it and then immediately written it off as an almost insignificant possibility.

'Look, it's far from definite yet, but I've been asked to go for an initial interview in London, so I'm going to go away for a few days and I might need you to step in and do the overnights with the kids for a bit.'

'Have you mentioned it to them yet?'

'I just told them I was going to visit an old friend. I don't want them worrying if it comes to nothing.' Josh looked uncomfortable. 'If I even get offered the job, then we can talk about what we might do. But when I say that this is a *once-in-a-lifetime* job, I really mean it. There will be hundreds of people who'd sell their granny to head up a project working on the Tubbataha Reef in the Philippines; it's akin to winning the lottery in my field of work. And given that all I've done for more than a year is to project manage a couple of small-scale studies from home, I really don't think it's worth worrying about too much yet. But you understand why I had to apply, don't you?'

'I do. Pete was always so proud of your conservation work, and if you do get the chance, I know he'd want you to take it. We talked about your work and how it isn't always a fit for family life when he asked if I'd be okay with being named in the will as joint-guardian, so I can't just pick and choose the aspects I signed up to.' Alasdair caught Josh's eye for a second. 'Even if none of us thought we'd ever really need to step up to that job, either.'

'I think we've done okay for the past year. The kids are both doing really well, and I haven't burned the house down yet!'

'They're great kids, aren't they?' Despite the burden of having to try and fill their parents' shoes, talking about Rory and Bronte never failed to make Alasdair smile. 'Where are they, by the way?'

'They're at a birthday party in the soft play centre for one of their child-minder's other children; she's bringing them back after. So you've no excuses not to tell me a whole lot more about the delectable Dr. Daniels.'

'What are you expecting me to say? That I made a move the moment she arrived?'

'No, but you want to, don't you?' Josh gave him a knowing look.

'She's quite brilliant.' Alasdair still didn't want to say anything that might make a comparison with Peter, but he couldn't tell Josh about Evie without using those words. She'd had more drama in the two days she'd been in town than they'd seen for a long time, but nothing seemed to overwhelm her. Maybe whatever it was that had driven her on the road, as she put it, had given her a protective shell too. 'Did you hear about the incident on the railway crossing yesterday?'

'Susie phoned me last night to get an update on how the children are doing.

She said you were the hero of the hour.' Josh raised an eyebrow and Alasdair laughed again. It was one of the things he'd loved most about Peter, the way he could bring Alasdair back down to earth with just a look, and it seemed as if Josh had the same knack.

'Evie was just driving into town, and she got caught up in the whole incident. She handled it like an absolute pro.' He smiled at the memory; that first look into those killer blue eyes of hers, and the way she'd bristled when he'd accused her of interfering in stuff she knew nothing about. She was sexy even when she was on the defensive. 'Then today we had two boys come into the surgery. They'd both swallowed plastic building bricks after a dare that went wrong. The youngest one was choking and he passed out. By the time I got to Evie, she'd already managed to clear his airway and got him breathing again. Then, when his older brother started to choke too and I had to perform a tracheotomy, she just coped with everything, even keeping the little one calm. I don't know, maybe the clinic she worked at down in London had those sort of emergencies every day, but I get the impression she could deal with anything.'

'In that case, ask her out. What's the worst that can happen? After all, she's already dealt with one train wreck!' Josh laughed at his own joke.

'Maybe I would, but she's made it clear that she's just passing through.'

'Well, that could be a bonus, if things don't work out.'

Alasdair didn't say what was on his mind — that life was too complicated right now as it was. Spending time with the children, when he could, and waiting for the inevitable day when Josh decided to take one job or another that meant he'd leave Balloch Pass, and he and Alasdair would have to try and make the right decision for Rory and Bronte. Even thinking about it over-whelmed him sometimes, and the last thing he wanted to do was to add another problem into the mix. Something about Evie told him she'd get under his skin if he let her; she definitely wasn't a candidate for a casual fling, even if Alasdair had been in the market for one. Not following his basic instincts and getting to know her on a personal level was a regret he'd have to live with when Evie moved on, but much better than risking letting another person into his life whom he was destined to lose. There'd been far too much of that in Balloch Pass already.

4

Things were supposed to happen in threes, or so the old saying went, but that hadn't proved the case for Evie. After two thrilling days in Balloch Pass — which had seen high drama on the railway crossing and the choking incident on her first day in the surgery — things had quietened down considerably.

It was now her second week in the job and the there'd been nothing more dramatic than a fractured wrist, which she'd referred on to the nearest hospital that still had an emergency department. The hospital was a thirty-mile round trip from Balloch Pass, with a notoriously long wait time, so it was no wonder the mother of the patient — an accident-prone skateboarder — had wanted to be almost sure he really had broken his wrist before they set off.

Alasdair had been friendly when she'd first started, but he seemed to have backed off a bit after that day in the surgery when he'd told her he wanted to take her for a drink. He was prone to rushing off at the end of the day, and whoever it was he was rushing to, she must have been quite demanding. He looked worn out some mornings, and had been known to sport a grazing of stubble across his cheeks and down to his oh-so-masculine jawline. More than once in their twice-weekly practice meetings, she'd fought the urge to touch his face, her mind wandering to what that stubble might feel like under her fingertips. She was learning to live with the feelings, though. It was just a physical attraction, her brain's way of distracting her from the enormity of leaving her whole life behind in London. Like life in Balloch Pass, her attraction to Alasdair James was temporary, and she was determined not to read too much into it.

'I see my clinics are on the agenda again, Alasdair?' Julia Monkhouse, the surgery's practice nurse, was already in the meeting room behind reception when Evie followed Alasdair in. She was a formidable-looking woman in her later fifties, but seeing her with the patients it was obvious she had a heart of gold. Evie had questioned, as a locum, whether she should really be in on the meetings at all, but Alasdair insisted he'd value her input. Judging by the look on Julia's face, though, this particular meeting wasn't going to be much fun.

'We need to think about how best to spend the resources, and I know you're really keen to get this obesity clinic up and running, but I don't know what else you think we can sideline to fit it in?' Alasdair sounded world-weary and Evie wondered if there was trouble in paradise. If a woman was keeping him up all night, then surely he should be a bit happier about it?

'I know, tell me about it. I can't cut the number of asthma, family planning or antenatal clinics we run, but I still think we could drop down to one diabetes clinic a month and run a weight loss clinic instead.' Julia shot him a look that would stop traffic. 'And please don't call it an obesity clinic, it will put people off attending.'

'That's half the problem, though.' Alasdair didn't sound his normal self at all. His voice was tight and there was a muscle going in his cheek, just the way it had been the first day Evie had met him, when he'd clearly been angry with her. 'Edging around everyone's feelings to protect them from the truth doesn't help in the end. Maybe if they were told bluntly exactly what obesity is doing to them, and that the responsibility for all that lies at *their* door, there'd be no need for a clinic in the first place.'

'I agree to an extent.' Evie had barely sat down before getting drawn into what was becoming a heated debate, but Alasdair had asked for her opinion and he was going to get it. 'I still think that sometimes the softly, softly approach is the right way to go. You want people to be willing to walk through the door.'

'I'm just sick to death of treating people who are their own worst enemies. Some of these people come in moaning about their poor health that's all caused because of their own life choices, and I feel like telling them exactly what I think.' Alasdair turned towards Helen, and Evie saw the practice nurse's face visibly soften. There was something going on that Evie didn't know about, some unspoken understanding between them about why Alasdair felt so strongly, that left her feeling distinctly on the outside of things.

'Like I say, I can see your point.' Evie spoke as much to break the awkwardness of the silence as anything else. 'But surely prevention has to be better than cure? And let's face it, none of us are saints, we're all going to make an unhealthy decision or an unwise choice at some point, and not everyone finds it easy to break those habits just because they should.' For a moment, her thoughts drifted to her ex-fiancé, but she squashed them down just as quickly.

'You're right, I'm sorry.' Alasdair looked in her direction, as if he'd only just noticed she was there. 'Let's trial it for three months and see how it goes. We can replace one of the diabetes clinics with an obesi- . . . *weight loss* clinic, and take it from there. I want results, though, be warned; not just a lot of talking that has no impact.'

'Yes boss!' Julia gave a mock salute and then leant over to given Alasdair a hug. There was definitely something the practice nurse knew about Alastair's reaction that Evie didn't, and she didn't like it one bit.

* * *

At least Evie knew where she was with her patients. She was there to diagnose if they had something she could treat, soothe their worries if no treatment was required, or refer them on to a specialist if the issue was beyond the scope of her expertise. Colleagues were far more complicated. There was potential for a working relationship to become more than that — friendship, or something even deeper. But right now, Evie felt like the new girl at school again, an outsider who didn't understand any of the in-jokes and couldn't make sense of what was going on below the surface, making Alasdair blow hot and cold. She was relieved to be back in her consulting room with something else to think about, but the last patient of the morning was destined to put everything else into perspective.

'How are you?' Evie greeted the elderly couple with a smile. They were holding hands as they walked into the consulting room.

'The appointment's for Lucy, Doctor.' Mr. Henderson guided his wife to the chair nearest Evie and then sat down beside her, taking her hand in his again.

'What can I do for you today, Lucy?'

'Me? Nothing. I'm fine, thank you,

Doctor.' The old lady smiled and turned to her husband. 'Can we go now?'

'Not just yet, Luce.' Mr. Henderson shook his head. 'She's starting to get much more forgetful, Doctor, and I just wondered if there was anything you could give her, you know, to bring my old Lucy back.'

'Let's start with a few questions.' Evie wished it were as simple as just writing Mrs. Henderson a prescription. 'Who's the prime minister?'

'That bloody Thatcher, of course.' Lucy looked distinctly unimpressed at the thought.

'And what month is it?'

'March, I think . . . or it might be April.' Lucy's confusion was starting to distress her, and there was no need for Evie to ask any more questions.

'How can she not know it's September, Doctor?' Mr. Henderson looked close to tears.

'Stop talking about me as if I'm not here. I haven't lost all my marbles just yet!'

'No-one's suggesting you have.' Evie lay what she hoped was a reassuring hand on Mrs. Henderson's arm. 'We'll start with some blood tests. I'll book you in with our practice nurse, Julia, for those, just to rule out any other problems. And then we can refer you to the memory clinic for some more detailed tests, so we can see where we're at and what support they can offer.'

'Thank you, Doctor. I don't think I could stand it if Lucy forgot who I was.'

'As if I'm going to forget the man I've been married to for over twenty years.' Mrs. Henderson shook her head. 'Men!'

'*Fifty* years.' Mr. Henderson said the words so quietly that Evie doubted his wife had even heard them, but the look on his face said so much more.

'And how are you?' Evie waited until Mr. Henderson's eyes met hers and he shook his head. 'It's really important that you get some support too. There are lots of organisations which have been set up to support carers, and there are often benefits you can have access to, as well as vouchers for complementary therapies, like massages, which might help you to look after yourself whilst you're so busy supporting Lucy. They also have counsellors available too, if you just need to talk to someone.'

'Sometimes that's all I want. To talk to someone who knows what it's like and really understands.' Mr. Henderson sighed as his wife caught hold of his elbow.

'Are we going now?' Mrs. Henderson frowned, determined not to take no for an answer this time.

'I'll have a look into what you might be entitled for at the moment, and I can either give you a call or send the information out to you. Then, once Lucy's had her tests, we can look at that side of things again too.' As Evie spoke, Mr. Henderson took her hand and squeezed it gently.

'Thanks so much, Doctor. I feel like there's a bit of hope now, whatever the outcome.'

It was heartbreaking, and even though she was determined to do whatever she could to help them both, there was no magic wand she could wave to make things right for them, however much she wanted to. Sometimes being a doctor wasn't all it was cracked up to be.

* * *

Alasdair was on his way to speak to Evie, to apologise for the way he'd acted at the practice meeting. Of course he had sympathy for people who found the lifestyle choices they'd made difficult to break. He shouldn't be a doctor if he couldn't have empathy for people, even when he didn't condone their actions. It was just, since the accident, it was hard to hear about people who were still choosing to smoke or others slowly eating themselves into an early grave. Pete had only been a social drinker, his only other vice was cheating at card games, and he'd been the perfect family man, as well as going for a five-mile run at least three times a week. Isabella had put her all into family life too, and made sure they all ate home-cooked meals every night. It wasn't fair that their lives should be cut so short, but that didn't mean Alasdair should use that as an excuse for going on a personal crusade. Julia had understood it was about Peter and Isabella, but he'd seen the way Evie had looked at him, and he owed her an explanation at the very least.

'Are you alright?' He'd been about to knock on the door of her consulting room when Evie had emerged, her blue eyes lacking their usual irresistible sparkle. Something had changed, maybe because of the way he'd been acting. Perhaps she'd decided to move on after the things he'd said this morning. She clearly thought he was far too judgemental, the sort of doctor who should have changed vocation years ago. He'd met enough of those types during his career.

'I'm fine. I just had a bit of a tricky

consultation, that's all.'

'Anything I can help with?'

'Mr. and Mrs. Henderson. It looks like she might have dementia, and he's devastated and exhausted.' She shrugged, as if she was trying to convince herself that Mrs. Henderson was just one more patient, but her face gave the game away. She cared, a lot, and that made her just the sort of doctor Balloch Pass needed.

'All you can do is be there to support them and refer them for whatever help there is.'

'I know, but sometimes that just doesn't seem like enough, does it?'

'It doesn't, so that's why it's important that we talk to each other when these sorts of things happen. You need somewhere to offload your feelings from time to time in this job, and I'm your man.' The words were out of his mouth before he'd had a chance to think them through, but if Evie had thought anything of the remark, she wasn't showing it.

'I was just thinking the same, funnily

enough, as they left the surgery — that only another doctor would really understand how it had left me feeling, so I was hoping I'd have the chance to talk to you about it. Can I do the same for you — if you ever need to talk, that is?'

'Actually, do you want to go for a walk? There *is* something I need to explain to you, and you look like you could do with some air.'

'I . . . ' She held his gaze for a moment, looking as if she wanted to turn down his suggestion of a walk, but then seemed to shake herself, remembering the offer she'd just made. 'Like I said, if you need to talk, then I'm here.'

'I do.'

When they got outside, Alasdair followed the path that led to the back of the surgery and opened out into a footpath which meandered downhill through the centre of St Radigan's Farm. It was a well-used track with a good layering of loose stone, which at this time of year was as solidly compacted as tarmac, so there shouldn't be too much danger of it ruining Evie's shoes. It was wide enough for them to walk side by side in companionable silence, but neither of them seemed in the mood to do so.

'Look, are you going to ask me to leave?' Evie turned to face him suddenly. 'I know the fact that I can't commit to staying for a set period makes me a less than ideal candidate, but I'm really enjoying working here.'

'Absolutely not! I hope I've made it clear that we'd welcome you staying on at the surgery until you feel you have to move on.' He still hadn't quite given up hope of her changing her mind on that front.

'So what is it you want to get off your chest?'

'It's nothing major. I just wanted to say that I'm sorry about this morning. You must have thought some of the things I said about the weight loss clinic were pretty heartless.'

'You did come on a bit strong at one point, but I can understand some of your frustration.' There was far less fight in her voice than there'd been earlier in the day. 'I just think, as doctors, if we come across as one more person judging the patient for what they've done in the past, rather than trying to help them, who on earth can they turn to for support?'

'You're right.' He took a deep breath, this next bit wasn't going to be easy, but he had to make her understand why he was so uptight. 'You might have noticed that I've been heading off from the surgery early some days, and I'm sorry if I've seemed to be in too much of a hurry to talk to you properly since you arrived.'

'That's okay. What you get up to after work is none of my business, and Susie and Julia have both been brilliant with giving me any information I needed.'

'You asked me about your predecessor when you first started.' As Alasdair spoke, she turned to look at him and nodded her head. 'I find it difficult to talk about Peter in the past tense, even though it's been over a year since his death. He was killed in an accident with his wife, and although they live with their uncle, I've just been trying to do everything I can to help Rory and Bronte, his children, since they lost their parents. And sometimes I just get so angry that other people are risking their lives by making stupid decisions that could so easily be avoided.'

'Oh, no; I'm so sorry.' Evie put her hand on his arm and, as he looked into her eyes, it was there — a sense of understanding he hadn't seen before. She didn't need to say anything else for him to know she'd lost someone she loved too, but when she did he was left in no doubt. 'It's so hard, sometimes, isn't it? There are some things that you'd give absolutely anything to solve as a doctor that you can't and it hurts all the more when people won't take the help or advice you can offer.'

'It sounds as if you're speaking from experience about problems you can't solve?' She was so close now he could smell the subtle aroma of her perfume — sweet and sensual as if it had been made for Evie herself.

'My mother died of a complication of Lyme Disease at the beginning of the year. Her GP dismissed her initial symptoms as a virus, and he didn't order any follow-up tests until it was far too late. She was eventually seen by several different consultants, and it took ages to get the diagnosis — it had damaged her heart too badly to be managed by then, and so we knew it was just a matter of time. I went with her for the initial consultation, and I'll never stop blaming myself for not pushing harder for those tests from the start.'

'I'm so sorry.' He swept a strand of golden-blonde hair away from her face, every part of him fighting the urge to kiss her. He wanted to, more than he could remember ever wanting to kiss someone, but it couldn't have been more inappropriate. She was grief-stricken, and he was supposed to be explaining why the children were his priority, not kissing those rosebud-pink lips which had a habit of drifting into his thoughts.

'I'm sorry about Peter and his wife, too. I think our experiences on the other side of the stethoscope colour the way we do our job, whether we want them to or not.' Evie looked up at him again, and he almost had to take a step back to curb the desire it provoked. He tried to concentrate on what she was saying instead, as she carried on: 'I think the unfairness of it all hits home when you see patients who could improve their health by taking your advice, but refusing to do so, when there are people like the Hendersons who can't do anything about what they're facing.'

'I wanted to tell you before about Peter and Isabella, but sometimes the easiest way to cope with it is not to talk about it, especially with new people.' He wasn't quite ready to tell her yet about the promise he'd made to his oldest friend, which might soon see him taking over all the responsibility from Josh. It was something he was still trying to get his head around. 'He was my partner in the practice and my best friend, which is why I've only been able to consider locums since the accident. After all, how do you replace your best friend?' It was a question Alasdair still couldn't bear to contemplate.

'You can't. Sometimes you just have to up sticks and try somewhere new instead, when your old world *without them* becomes a place you can't stand to be any more.' She squeezed his hand again, and it was as though a pulse of electricity had shot through him. Life really wasn't playing fair. If he'd met her at any other time, he wouldn't have held back. He wanted to get to know this woman with the amazing blue eyes, the most kissable lips he'd ever seen, and a history that seemed to connect them on a deeper level. Only it wasn't another time. He could fall for her in an instant, but he couldn't let that happen.

His only chance was to step back and put up the wall he'd only just taken down. Disentangling his hand, he forced a smile and gestured back towards the surgery.

'Thanks for being so understanding.' Adopting a professional tone, he forced the intimacy of the last ten minutes back where it belonged: in the same place he'd kept his attraction to Evie since the first time he'd seen her — locked up tight. 'I guess we'd better be heading back.'

'Of course.' There was confusion in her voice, no doubt because he'd changed tack so suddenly. 'But I hope you know where I am if you need me?'

'Thank you.' The words were bland but he didn't trust himself to say anything else. He didn't *need* Evie, he *wanted* to be with her, but that was far too dangerous a feeling to acknowledge. So he swallowed hard and walked back to the surgery, a new heaviness in his step.

5

Life in Balloch Pass had started to settle into something that felt familiar — comfortable, even. Most of the patients had only minor ailments, and there hadn't been any more of the drama that she'd seen in the early days of her arrival. It was one of those places that had slightly overgrown its original status as a village, but which definitely put the *small* in its small-town description. The only tension that existed was between her and Alasdair. There was an undercurrent of attraction there that she couldn't deny no matter how hard she tried. She wasn't normally given to overconfidence, but she'd have bet her last pound that he felt it too, but he was fighting it just as hard as she was. Sometimes she caught him looking at her with an intensity that took her breath away, but then he seemed to shut off altogether. Since he'd told her about Peter and Isabella's accident, he'd gone back to keeping their conversations strictly professional. There was a good chance he regretted opening up to her at all, but she missed the friendship that had been seeming to grow between them. It was for the best, though; they both knew her days in Balloch Pass were numbered and it would be far easier to leave with things on the cordial terms they were now. It didn't stop her dreaming about Alasdair sometimes, but if her subconscious decided to let her down, there really wasn't much she could do about that.

Expecting another routine afternoon at the surgery, Evie breezed through her first five appointments after lunch, but she hadn't anticipated the issues that seeing the next patient would rake up for her too.

'I think I've got an infected insect bite, Doctor. I live near the edge of the loch and the midges always seems to come out in force at this time of year, just before it starts to cool down. So I've had plenty of bites before, but this one's different, and it's really red and uncomfortable.' Maddie Harris sat with her toddler son perched awkwardly on her knee, the little boy straining to get down as his mother turned towards Evie. 'It seems to have got quite a bit bigger since I first found it.'

'When did you first notice it?' Evie looked back at Maddie's notes on the screen in front of her. She hadn't been in to the surgery for over two years, since just after her little boy was born. Even though Evie knew there was only a tiny chance of the bite being caused by a tick, and even less chance of it developing into Lyme Disease, she could feel her hand shaking.

'About a week or ten days ago, I suppose. I thought it might just run its course.' Maddie bit her lip and Evie hoped she wasn't picking up on her panic.

'Have you had any symptoms?' She ran through the list with her patient.

The potential symptoms of Lyme Disease were now etched on her brain. Even if she hadn't been a doctor, she would have known them inside out.

'Like I said there's just a bit of redness over the lump and it's really painful around the area.' Maddie managed a half-smile, which Evie still couldn't bring herself to mirror.

Do you mind if I examine you?'

Maddie set her son on the floor and produced a couple of toys for him from the bag she'd brought with her.

'It's on my ribcage, Doctor. Shall I just lift my top up?'

'It would probably be better if I examined you lying down. Would you like me to ask the practice nurse to come in?'

Maddie shook her head and followed Evie's instructions, the angry-looking red lump visible immediately. Aware of Maddie's eyes on her as she began her examination, she tried not to give anything away in her expression.

'I'm sure it's nothing and I don't

really know why I bothered to come in. I hardly ever need to come to the doctor's and all the women in my family live to be a grand old age.' Maddie was speaking very quickly, as if she was trying to convince herself, and Evie, that the whole thing was a waste of time. 'My great-granny only died last year, but she had a pretty big stroke five years before. She swore blind it was only Dr. James's care and attention that got her through and made sure she got her letter from the Queen. She had three years more on top of that.'

'It's always best to check with your doctor if you've got any concerns about symptoms you are having, so please don't worry that you're wasting any-one's time.' Evie had a vague awareness of sounding robotic, as if she had gone onto autopilot, suddenly unable to trust the first diagnosis that came into her head. It had all the hallmarks of a simple infected insect bite, there were no other symptoms to suggest Lyme Disease. Antibiotics and a bit of watching and waiting was the right course of action. She was ninety-nine point nine percent sure of it, but there was a voice screaming in her head: *What if . . . ?* Sometimes being almost certain just wasn't enough.

'Would you mind if I examined your neck to check the glands there?' Evie's hands were shaking again, her eyes darting towards where the little boy sat playing with his toys. If she got this wrong, there could be so many implications.

'Of course.' Maddie was twisting her wedding ring round and Evie so wanted to reassure her that in all likelihood the infection would simply respond to a course of tablets, but she couldn't say it. What if she was wrong and it was too late by the time the symptoms became obvious? Alasdair had told her to call on him if she needed him, and she didn't care if this was stupid, she had to get this double-checked.

'I don't think this is anything to . . . ' Evie couldn't bring herself to offer even a tentative reassurance. 'But I think it would be really useful if Dr. James could give us a second opinion, just so that I can be certain.'

'Okay. I really thought you'd just tell me to get some over-the-counter cream.' Sitting up on the examination couch, Maddie pulled down her top.

Evie shook her head, doing her best to offer a noncommittal smile. She'd been on the receiving end of those sort of dismissals before, though, when she'd been there to support her mum, and the obvious diagnosis didn't always turn out to be the right one. 'I'll be right back with Dr. James.'

Evie stood outside Alasdair's door for a few seconds, trying to hear whether he was in with a patient and almost got knocked off her feet as the door suddenly opened and a middle-aged man came out, calling out a thank-you to Alasdair as he did.

'Have you got a moment before your next patient, please?' Evie stepped inside his consultation room and braced herself for how he might react when he knew why. If she couldn't deal with an insect bite without going into a panic, what use could she be to him?

'Of course, I'll just let them know in Reception. What's the problem?'

'I've got a patient with what looks like an infected insect bite, only I'm worried that I might miss something and make the wrong call.' Evie bit her lip, desperate to retain some vestige of professionalism and absolutely refusing to become tearful. 'I'm sorry, I know I should be able to trust myself on this, it's just . . . '

'It's not a problem at all.' Alasdair stood up and looked at her in that intense way he had. 'I'll just let them know to hold off on my next patient for a few minutes.'

Evie slowed her pace back to her consulting room. She didn't want to see Maddie again without Alasdair. She couldn't bear the young mother's need for the reassurance she just didn't feel able to give. Alasdair caught up with her just as she reached the door.

'You know Dr. James, don't you, Maddie?'

'Yes, very well. I was just telling Dr. Daniels how my great grandmother used to sing your praises.' Maddie was sitting on the examination table, her little boy thankfully still occupied with his favourite toys.

'Good to see you again, Maddie.' Alasdair's tone was warm and immediately reassuring, to Evie at least. It was no wonder his patients loved him so much. 'Do you mind if I just examine you quickly, so Dr. Daniels and I can be sure that it's nothing to worry about?'

'Go for it, I'd much rather ten people had a look, if it means I can be certain it's nothing horrible.'

Alasdair repeated the examination and questions that Evie had asked moments before.

'Well the good news is, Maddie, I agree with Dr. Daniels that it looks like it's nothing too much to worry about.' Alasdair smiled, and Evie could have kissed him there and then. Judging by the look that crossed Maddie's face, she wasn't the only one.

'Now that we've got that confirmation, we can treat the infection with a course of antibiotics, which should resolve the pain and stop the infection spreading.' Evie felt her shoulders relax, unaware until that moment just how tensely she'd been holding herself. 'I'm sorry I had to get a second opinion, but I just wanted to be completely sure.'

'Not at all, Doctor; like I said, I'd much rather you did that.' Maddie stood up and scooped up her son who, having finally tired of his toys, was playing with the cuff of the blood pressure monitor.

'Just let us know if you're concerned about anything or if the symptoms haven't reduced by the end of the course of antibiotics.' Evie handed her patient the prescription.

'Will do, Dr. Daniels, and thank you both again.' With a wriggling toddler on one hip, Maddie left the consulting room and Evie held her breath, waiting for Alasdair to tell her not to waste his time like that again.

'Are you okay?' He put his hand on her arm instead, that intense look back on his face.

'I'm sorry, I know I should be able to cope with that sort of thing, but it's the first patient like that I've had to deal with since Mum died.'

'Don't be sorry, I completely understand how everything that happened with your mum has affected you. The fact that you care so much about your patients and getting things right is just one of your many qualities.' He took a step towards her.

'My *many* qualities?' She suddenly wanted more than anything to hear what he thought they were.

'So, so many. I could start with your beautiful smile, but if I focus on your lips then I'm not sure I'll get any further.' He was inches away now, and she was having to fight the urge to throw her arms around his neck.

'Why don't you try it and see how you get on?'

'If you insist, Doctor.' His voice was low and husky, and as his lips finally met hers, it was as if there was an unbreakable connection between them. Her hands met at the back of his neck and he was holding her around the waist. If he'd asked her *anything* at the moment, she'd have been powerless to refuse. Except for the one thing he did ask, as he finally pulled away:

'Are you sure I can't persuade you to stay in Balloch Pass?' There was a teasing tone in his voice, and she so wanted to say yes, but she just couldn't. There were other promises that needed to be fulfilled first.

'It's not that I don't want to. Being around you is something I could definitely get used to.' She was tempted just to kiss him again, to try and make him forget the question, but he was already moving further away from her.

'But?'

'When my mother knew she was

dying, she made me promise I'd do some of the things she never had, and that I'd see the world before I met someone and settled down.' It sounded almost ridiculous saying it out loud, but the plan had been a bond between Evie and her mother, something that would keep her in Evie's life even after she was gone.

'What if life throws you a curveball, though? You can't always choose when you're going to meet the people who are going to be important to you.'

'I can't let it change my plans, I made her a promise to live life to the full, and . . . '

'Life in Balloch Pass just doesn't cut it?' He cut her off before she had a chance to finish, his tone cool. 'I think I've kept my next patient waiting far too long already.'

'Alasdair, I really do like you. If it was any other time . . . '

'But it's not, is it? If you're going soon, then at least we both know where we stand.' He shut the door of the consulting room behind him and Evie slumped against the desk. She wanted to give being with Alasdair a chance more than almost anything; but, for the second time that day, she realised that *almost* just wasn't enough.

*   *   *

By the end of the afternoon, Evie had decided she should speak to Alasdair about it. If you could lose someone you loved to illness, or even to a sudden accident, then why worry so much about the future? Alasdair clearly wasn't the settling-down type — he'd got to his mid-thirties without a divorce or even a live-in relationship behind him, from what she could gather. Yet the thought of him filled her head every time she had a spare moment, and she couldn't let herself think about the kiss. There was no denying the attraction and if how long she was staying really was the only issue, she couldn't understand the problem. If she was

102

prepared to risk falling in love with him and having to leave, then why wasn't he? After all, given his track record, it was much more likely she'd end up being the one who found it hardest to walk away.

Heading out to Reception, she was hoping to catch him to suggest they had a chat, but instead she was met by a very worried-looking Susie who was pacing up and down behind her reception desk.

'Are you okay, Susie?' Evie virtually had to put her hands on the other woman's arms to keep her still.

'Yes, no, I've just had a call from Josh to say that Rory's asthma is playing up, and his inhaler's run out and they can't find the spare anywhere.' She grimaced. 'Josh doesn't really want to call an ambulance because it's not that bad at the moment, but he's got no car either, and there's no way Rory's up to walking over here.'

'Where's Alasdair?'

'Out on a home visit, and Julia's got a

clinic, so I've got to be here to sign the patients in, and I don't drive anyway.'

'I've got my car back at the hotel. It will only take me five minutes to walk over there and pick it up.'

'Are you sure you don't mind?' Relief flooded Susie's face as she spoke. 'Only I don't know how long Alasdair's going to be out. Josh isn't prone to panicking, but . . . '

'Of course I don't mind. Rory obviously needs an inhaler quickly, and I'm more than happy to take it.' Evie grabbed a piece of paper and a pen off Susie's desk. 'If you can just tell me how to get to their house, I'll head straight over.'

* * *

Thankfully the house, on the outskirts of the town, wasn't too difficult to find. Evie knew from experience that even satnavs could get themselves lost in the outreaches of Balloch Pass and, with autumn arriving, the days were getting shorter. So it would have been far more of a challenge to find his place if he'd lived somewhere remote.

Pulling up outside the house, Evie took a deep breath as she pushed open the car door. They were obviously a family who'd suffered unimaginable tragedy, and she wondered if that would fill the atmosphere inside. As a doctor, she was supposed to separate out the emotion from a situation, except that was often a lot harder to do than it sounded.

Pressing the bell, she waited for about thirty seconds until the door was drawn back with so much enthusiasm it was almost pulled off its hinges.

'Are you Dr. Daniels? Susie rang to tell us you were coming with Rory's medicine.' A little girl with two very haphazard plaits trailing down towards her shoulders greeted her with a smile. 'I'm Bronte.'

'Nice to meet you.' Evie suppressed a smile as the little girl held out her hand, a very grown-up expression on her face.

'And I'm five, but I'll be six soon.' Bronte imparted the second piece of information with the importance it deserved.

'That's one of the best ages to be.' Evie gave into the smile this time round. 'Where are Rory and your Uncle Josh?'

'In the kitchen. Rory's breathing in the freezer air.'

Evie knew that asthmatics often found it easier to breathe cold air when they felt an attack was coming on, and Josh was obviously an old hand at managing the little boy's symptoms too.

'Uncle Josh is making us something disgusting for dinner!' Bronte pulled a face as she led Evie into the kitchen.

'Bronte! What she means is, I'm putting vegetables in it.' Josh, who had his hand on Rory's shoulder, turned to look at them both. 'Rory seems to be managing his breathing like a trooper, but I didn't really want him to move away from the freezer until we had the inhaler.' He took the inhaler from

Evie's outstretched hand, giving it to his nephew, who expertly self-administered the medication. 'Thanks so much for driving it over.'

'It was my pleasure.' Evie could already see the colour in Rory's face going back to normal, and he pushed the fridge door shut. 'Can I just take a quick look at you please, Rory, to make sure we don't need to do anything else?'

'If you like.' He shrugged. 'But this happens all the time and I feel fine as soon as I take my medicine. It wasn't even that bad this time. Once Mum had to go in the ambulance with me to the hospital, all the blue lights flashing and everything.'

'Well, it sounds like you're a pro, and your breathing and pulse both seem normal now.' Evie struggled to keep her voice even; he was an amazing boy, able to talk about the mum he'd lost a little over a year before without crying. She was a grown woman and could still barely manage that.

'You're even prettier than Uncle

Alasdair said.' Rory widened his eyes as Evie laughed in response. 'Oops, I wasn't supposed to tell you that!'

They were fantastic kids, she could see that already. Bronte had a personality as big as a house, despite her tiny stature, and Rory seemed so grown-up, managing his asthma with the sort of calmness that most adults couldn't manage. It was so unfair that they'd been through so much in their lives already.

'It's nice to meet you properly, by the way, Dr. Daniels; although, as my nephew says, we've already heard a lot about you. And there's no use trying to keep secrets if you're going to let an eight-year-old boy in on them!' Whatever it was Josh was cooking smelt far more delicious than Bronte had described.

'Call me Evie, please, all of you. And I'm sure I've heard much more about you.'

'All good, I hope?' Josh smiled.

'Definitely all good.' Evie reached into her bag. 'I've brought a couple more spare inhalers, just in case — do you want me to put them somewhere for you?'

'No, it's fine, I can take them upstairs.' He shot a glance in the children's direction. 'Look, can I have a real cheek and ask you just to keep an eye on this risotto whilst I nip upstairs with the medicine? Bronte's dying to taste it — aren't you, angel? — and I wouldn't want it getting stuck to the pan so I'd have to give her chicken nuggets instead!'

'Please let it burn, Evie!' Bronte was suddenly clinging to her arm in an attempt to stop her moving closer to the stove.

'Come on, let's both keep an eye on it for your Uncle Josh. It smells fantastic, and if you can forget about the vegetables for a bit, I'm sure you'll really like it.'

By the time Josh had come back downstairs, Evie had been coerced into promising the children a game of Uno before she left. She chatted with Josh too, finding out more about his brother's long-standing friendship with Alasdair, and Josh's work as a marine biologist that had taken him all over the world. She had the sense that he was far from done with globetrotting, and she couldn't help wondering how he'd manage that now he'd taken on his brother's children. She could imagine being friends with Josh, but there was no attraction between them, unlike the thunderbolt she felt every time she looked at Alasdair, which meant she had even less reason to try and dismiss her feelings for her new boss — something else to worry about.

In the end, Bronte persuaded her to stay for dinner, with a promise that she would at least try the risotto if Evie had some too. They were just finishing off their meal when Alasdair walked into the kitchen.

'Susie told me you'd come over, but I didn't expect to find you still here.' He narrowed his eyes slightly, and Evie experienced that now-familiar flutter at the sight of him. Although he didn't look remotely pleased to see *her*.

'This woman is even more amazing than you said.' Josh laughed. 'She managed to get Bronte — *our* Bronte — to eat some vegetables.'

'I'll admit that is quite something.' Alasdair scooped the little girl into his arms. 'But I'm sure Evie's got other things she wants to do this evening, and I'm here to keep an eye on Rory's asthma now.'

'But she said we could have another game of Uno after dinner. And I'm fine, look — I'm even cleaning up.' Rory, who was already clearing the plates, looked up at Alasdair with a sullen expression on his face.

'I can do that too. Poor Evie doesn't want to hang around here all night.' Alasdair gave her a look, as if daring her to contradict him.

'Maybe we can have another game some other time?' She squeezed Rory's shoulder. 'I'm really glad you're feeling better, but I probably should be getting off anyway.'

'Thank you for a lovely evening.' Josh stood up at the same time as her and leant over to kiss her cheek. 'And thanks for bringing the medicine over, too; you're an angel. Don't be a stranger, okay?'

Evie nodded and swallowed hard. She'd have loved to spend some more time with the children, especially with Alasdair there. But he'd made it clear that was the last thing he wanted.

'I'll see you to the door — and I'm seriously hoping, Josh, that you've saved some of that risotto to warm up for me?' Alasdair set Bronte down and followed Evie along the corridor. She turned to face him as she reached the door.

'I wanted to talk to you about this afternoon.' She didn't mention the kiss, but it must have been obvious what she meant. She searched for the look in his eyes she'd seen so many times before, but it was as if someone had painted a mask on, his face completely impassive.

'I think it's probably best if we just

forget it, don't you? With you moving on soon, you can see how complicated life is here for me right now. I need to be around to help Josh with the kids, and none of us need someone else to get close to who's just going to walk out.'

'That makes sense.' Evie pushed her speech about living for the moment back down her throat. She could see his point, and maybe he was right — maybe it was unfair of her to think everyone else should live in the moment just because that's what she decided to do. Pulling the door closed behind her, she was enveloped in the cool night air, and by the time she got back to her car, she was shivering.

⋆   ⋆   ⋆

'Are you an *actual* idiot?' Josh put a plate of risotto in front of Alasdair as he spoke. The children had gone off in search of the Operation board game, which Alasdair had promised to play with them in lieu of their second game of Uno with Evie.

'What?' Alasdair knew exactly what he meant, but he wasn't going to admit it.

'Virtually shoving Evie out the door like that! It couldn't be more obvious that you like her — and I mean *really* like her — if you stamped it on your forehead. So what's your problem?'

'She's moving on. She can't stay in Balloch Pass long because of some promise she made to her mother not to settle down too soon. This part of the world is never going to be enough for her, and I just don't have the energy right now to get into something that's just going to cause more drama in the end.'

'Because of the kids?'

'Of course not.' It was a blatant lie, and Alasdair pushed some of the rice around with his fork, his appetite completely gone. 'It's just ... seeing her with them, I don't want them getting to know her and like her, only to have her walk out on them.'

'You think, because of what happened to their mum and dad? Come on, Alasdair, that's rubbish. As nice as Evie is, having her leave Balloch Pass is barely going to register with the kids in comparison. But tonight, she had them both giggling over a game of cards, and she got Bronte to eat something I never thought she'd touch. They were having fun tonight. Not everything has to be tied up in the future. What happened to Pete and Issy should have taught you that. Have a bit of fun; live a bit for now and grab life, my friend.'

'Has anyone ever told you that you should go into counselling with your skills?' Alasdair couldn't help laughing at the self-righteous expression on Josh's face. Although he wondered if part of it was Josh laying a bit more groundwork for taking up his dream job if he was offered it.

'Funnily enough, no.'

'I can't see why.'

'Will you at least promise to think

about what I said? One of us needs to have some fun.' There was that edge to Josh's voice again: he was obviously struggling with life in Balloch Pass, maybe even more than Evie.

'I'll think about it.' Alasdair pushed another forkful of rice towards the edge of his plate. Maybe Josh was right, but he couldn't help feeling it would be better if he and Evie went back to just being friends. Someone like her was too much of a risk. He only hoped friendship was something she still wanted and that she wasn't already back at the hotel, packing her bags to leave Balloch Pass for good.

6

Falling for Alasdair James would have been an easy mistake for Evie to make. He was undeniably good-looking, and at times he made her feel as if she were the only woman in the world, never mind the room. It was his habit of blowing hot and cold that kept her guard up, though. Just when she thought they were getting close to something that might blur the lines of their professional relationship once and for all, he seemed to close down again and take a step away from her. There was a big risk he could break her heart if she let him, and a little part of it had fragmented when he'd pushed her away that night she'd taken Rory's inhaler over. He'd more or less told her he regretted their kiss and had decided to keep things strictly professional from here on out, so it came as something of a surprise when he asked to take her out for coffee after work one Friday afternoon.

All day she'd been worrying about why he wanted to see her. Maybe he was going to say that things weren't working out at the surgery after all, despite his previous reassurances. He obviously didn't want to take things further, even though she'd lit up like a Christmas tree every time he looked at her. She didn't want to feel that way, but she seemed to have lost control of her senses since that kiss.

She had one more appointment before she finished for the day. As far as she was concerned, this patient could take as long as they liked. She was in no rush to meet up with Alasdair and hear him say he didn't want her as a colleague any longer, never mind anything else.

'I think she's got another ear infection, Doctor.' Candy Ryan's mother had barely got through the door of Evie's consulting room before providing her own diagnosis of her daughter's condition. A quick glance at Candy's notes revealed that these infections were becoming an increasingly common occurrence, and the little girl winced in pain as Evie took out her otoscope.

'Okay sweetheart, I know you're in pain, but I just need to take a quick look in your ears. Hold Mummy's hand and try to sit still just for a couple of seconds while I see what's causing the problem.' Candy screwed up her face, but did as she was told, squeezing her mum's hand so tightly that the knuckles on her hand turned white.

'Is it another infection?' There was a sigh in her mother's voice and it was obviously difficult for her to see her daughter in so much discomfort.

'I'm afraid so. Has she been taking anything for the pain?'

'I've been giving her Calpol, but it doesn't last long enough between doses, and when I hear her cry out it's just awful.'

'I can imagine.' Evie did a quick

count-up of the number of ear infections Candy had suffered. She'd been into the surgery eight times over the past two years, and at only six years old it seemed she had a recurrent problem. 'You can give her children's ibuprofen alongside the Calpol, and if you use them intermittently, it should keep the pain under control. I also think it would be useful to repeat the steam inhalations that were recommended last time, and I'm going to prescribe some antibiotics to see if we can keep the glue ear at bay. If she does develop that again, though, I think we should perhaps consider surgery.' Evie almost mouthed the last word, so as not to frighten her young patient.

'That would be such a relief, Doctor.' Candy's mother smiled for the first time. 'My cousin went deaf on one side after getting glue ear lots of times as a kid, and I was really worried the same might happen to Candy.'

'It's a really simple procedure.' Evie was still being careful to avoid the word *operation*. 'So I'll make a referral to the hospital to put the wheels in motion, as unfortunately there's a waiting list. That way, if she does develop glue ear again — which it looks as though she might — we'll be a tiny bit further up that list. How does that sound?'

'Fantastic, Doctor, thank you.'

Evie handed Candy's mother the prescription and followed them out to Reception. It was time to face the music and find out exactly what it was Alasdair wanted to say. He was already out by the reception desk and she tried to read the expression on his face. Did he look like someone about to ask her how quickly she could move her stuff out of his surgery?

'You've got a good one here, Dr. James.' Candy's mother paused on her way out to address Alasdair. 'She's got empathy — believe me, I've seen a lot of doctors over the years, and not all of them have. She's like you: thorough, caring, and you want to keep hold of her if you can.'

'I'll do my best. And I'm glad you think Dr. Daniels is a good addition to the surgery, because I do too.' Alasdair smiled at the woman and Evie's shoulders relaxed. Surely he'd have given a noncommittal answer if he'd been planning to sack her? Whatever it was he wanted to talk to her about, it didn't sound as if it would involve him asking her to leave Balloch Pass before she was ready to. Either way, she was determined not to show him how much being near him affected her. If he wanted to keep things strictly business, then two could play at that game.

* * *

Candy Ryan's mother wasn't the only one who wanted Evie to say at the surgery permanently, Alasdair wanted it more than he could rationalise. It was obvious she was a good doctor, with the sort of bedside manner that put patients immediately at ease — something that couldn't be taught, no matter how many years were spent in training. She was a risk, too, and for that reason Alasdair knew he should want her to move on sooner rather than later. If he was being rational, he'd even have made sure of it.

The risk had nothing to do with her work, though, and everything to do with how she made him feel. He'd noticed things about her that a colleague really shouldn't: the way that her hair looked as though it was streaked with threads of gold when the sunlight caught it; the deep dimple that appeared in her right cheek when she smiled; not to mention the subtle scent of her perfume which always made him want to take a step closer to her. He'd never had this problem with a colleague before. Admittedly, there'd been a few short-term relationships with colleagues over the years, but none of them had presented the sort of risk that Evie did — the risk that it might go further, beyond something he could control and finish on his terms, as he always had. If he gave in to the feelings he had for her, he'd be relinquishing control; and with everything else he had going on in his life, it just wasn't a risk he could afford to take, despite what Josh had said about living for the moment. That didn't stop him waking up in the morning with her on his mind. So he wasn't quite sure why he was taking her out for coffee, and why he was about to make the suggestion he was. He could try to justify it by telling himself it was just an attempt to get a good locum to stay on for a bit longer, but he wasn't in the habit of lying to himself.

'I expect you're wondering why I asked you to come out for coffee?' Alasdair waited until they were at a table in the corner of Lovetts, an old-fashioned tearoom and coffee shop on the edge of Balloch Pass.

'I must admit, I was a bit worried at first that you might want to tell me things weren't working out with me at the surgery.' She looked up at him, the apprehension obvious in those striking blue eyes that got to him every time.

'No, nothing like that. Sorry, I should have said; it's quite the opposite, in fact.'

'So you brought me here to tell me that things are working out well in the surgery?'

'Not exactly. They are, but that's not why I wanted to bring you here. If you're willing to stay on as a locum for a few more months, until . . . ' He couldn't finish the sentence; he didn't need to. Evie knew he couldn't consider a permanent replacement for Peter yet, so there was no reason to pour salt into that open wound again and say it out loud. ' . . . until you're ready to move on, I wondered if you were happy to stay on at the pub for all that time? It must be difficult living out of one room.'

'It's not ideal, I'll admit, but rental properties want at least a six-month commitment, and that's just not some-thing I'm able to give.' Evie looked down slightly as she spoke, aware that her unwillingness to commit to the surgery was something he found difficult to understand, despite what she'd told him about her promise to her mother. She was fantastic with the patients, amazing in a crisis, and she would be the perfect candidate to stay long-term. She was close to perfect all round, but he couldn't acknowledge that.

'What about if I could offer you an alternative? A place you could rent on a month-by-month basis — or even week-by-week, if a month is too long-term?'

'I don't think renting a room in your house would be a good idea.'

'Me neither.' Alasdair couldn't stop the thought of her living in his house running through his head. 'Peter and I invested in a few holiday properties in and around the town: we bought the first one almost ten years ago now. They're always fully booked in the summer, with people wanting a base to go walking from, but at this time of year things quieten down a bit and there's a nice little one-bedroom cottage with its own garden that might suit you.'

'I hadn't thought of something like that, but I must admit it does get noisy, and I'm eating far too much pub food as a result of not having my own kitchen.' She hesitated for a moment. 'Are you sure you wouldn't be losing out, renting the place to me? I don't want to feel that I'll be leaving you in the lurch if I don't stay long-term, and you can't get any guests booked in until you know when I'm leaving. If it's easier, we could agree an exact date for me to leave now?'

'No.' He hadn't meant for his response to be as emphatic as it was, but he definitely didn't want Evie to set a date for her departure. The longer she stayed, the more chance he had of convincing that she could make the town her home. 'But I guess you might want to see the place before you commit to a decision?'

'That would probably be a good idea.'

'It's that one with the duck-egg-blue door, just across the road.' Alasdair gestured out of the window towards the Grade II-listed cottage, at the end of a terrace, almost immediately opposite the tearooms. He hadn't been able to resist buying it when it had gone on the market, and they'd never had any shortage of guests wanting to rent it, so he'd be surprised if its chocolate-box looks didn't win Evie over too.

'It's so cute!' She turned back from the cottage to look at him, her face shining. 'It's the sort of place my mum talked about retiring to. She was going to move out of London and have all that, a little cottage garden in the country somewhere with roses around the door.'

'I'm sorry, I didn't mean to upset you.' Against his better judgement, Alasdair reached out and placed his hand over hers, the reaction it stirred in him signalling that he'd been right to be cautious.

'You haven't upset me; in fact, it

helps. When she was in the last weeks of her life, she talked a lot about the things she didn't get to do, and each time I can tick one of them off, it feels a bit like she had the chance to do them after all. As long as you're happy to rent it to me not knowing when it will be vacant again, then I'd love to take it.'

'Don't you want to look inside first?' He'd taken his hand off hers, but his eyes kept being drawn back to her face. He didn't want to tell her that he'd rent her the house for nothing if it meant she'd stay on for longer; he couldn't afford to give in to his feelings any more than she could. They both had reasons for keeping a distance between them — call it self-preservation in its simplest terms — only he couldn't be entirely honest about his, even to himself; the prospect of what he was about to take on, and try to live up to, was just too huge.

'That would be lovely, but unless it's not fit for human habitation, I'm yours.' Her beautiful face suddenly flushed with colour. 'As a tenant, I mean, not . . . '

'It's alright, I know what you meant.' An unwanted image flashed through his mind again, but he forced a smile. Maybe he was a fool plotting ways to make Evie stay; it was going to be hard having her around and keeping his guard up, but the alternative of her walking away from Balloch Pass altogether seemed the far greater of two evils. 'Shall we go and take a look, then?'

★　★　★

Evie followed Alasdair across the road, trying not to notice the breadth of his shoulders and the way his jeans clung to his legs. This really hadn't been part of the plan, and suddenly a big part of her wanted Alasdair to have been that grey-haired doctor approaching retirement. Not a devastatingly handsome single guy in his mid-thirties who made her not want to worry about the consequences when the time came for her to move on from Balloch Pass. Sadly, that didn't seem to be enough for him.

Forcing herself to look up at the cottage as they got to the front door, she smiled. It was the wrong time of year for roses to be in bloom, but there was a trellis around the door bearing the spiky vines of a climbing rose. Her mother would definitely approve.

Alasdair led her on a guided tour of the house, which didn't take long. It was the definition of cosy, with a matching pair of two-seater leather sofas that flanked the open fireplace. There was a small kitchen at the back, with handmade wooden units and a beautiful scrubbed oak dresser taking up all of one wall. She had loads of pictures of her mum and life back in London that she hadn't been able to put up properly since she'd arrived in town. There were a couple of her favourites on the bedside table in her room at the pub, but she could already imagine them lined up on the dresser. It was guaranteed to make it feel like home.

Upstairs was a reasonably-sized room, dominated by a king-sized wooden sleigh bed, with wardrobes and a dressing table cleverly built into the alcove.

'Who did those? It's a fantastic use of the space, and there's everything here a girl could need.' She turned towards Alasdair, his dark eyes meeting hers, and her stomach did another involuntary flip.

'I made them.' He smiled, and she tried not to remember what it was like to kiss him, but it wasn't easy to forget. 'My father had a carpentry business before he and Mum retired to somewhere with sun; the Scottish weather seems to aggravate her arthritis. I spent hours watching him work when I was growing up, and I earned some decent money to help pay my way through uni using the skills he taught me. I actually enjoy doing it, and I've done a bit of work in all the houses Pete and I have bought.'

'Is there no end to your talents?' The

words had escaped from her lips before she had a chance to think them through properly. Being around Alasdair seemed to have that effect on her.

'Definitely. I'm a lousy cook, and I can't tell the difference between weeds and flowers. Before he died, Pete always took care of the gardens at the properties; and as for the cooking, I rely on pub food and ready meals far too much too. Thank goodness we're too far out to get takeaways delivered.'

'I love the cottage, so maybe I can repay you by cooking a meal to say thanks once I'm moved in?'

'That would be great. I'd love to return the offer, but the only meal I've ever really got the hang of cooking properly is a full Scottish breakfast.'

'That doesn't sound so bad.'

'Actually, it isn't; in fact, it's pretty amazing, even if I do say so myself.' He smiled, and there was that flutter in her stomach again.

'I can well believe it.' Evie spoke quietly and their eyes met again. Good intentions could only do so much, as Alasdair took a step towards her and she mirrored his action, until they were only inches apart. The tenderness in the kiss she'd waited so long to relieve left her almost breathless.

'Ignore it.' She whispered the words urgently as his phone began to ring. As a doctor, she knew how selfish it was to say that. Someone might need him! But she couldn't help it.

'I *want* to.' He was already drawing away from her, regret in his eyes. 'But you know I can't. If someone needs me . . . if it's Josh ringing about one of the kids, I just can't.'

'I know, I'm sorry, I should never had said that.' Evie was hot with guilt at the mention of the children. She'd never acted like this before, she always put other people first — especially her patients — but when it came to Alasdair, it was as if she turned into someone else altogether, someone who forgot about everyone but him.

'Alasdair James.' He took the call,

turning away from her slightly as he did so, and wedging the phone between his jaw and shoulder. 'Have you called an ambulance? I'm with Dr. Daniels now, so we'll both head up to the farm in the meantime, in case there's something we can do before they get there.'

'What is it?' Evie sagged with relief. If they were heading to a farm, at least that meant it was nothing to do with the children. A few seconds out of Alasdair's reach had given her back her clarity. They were doctors, and that always came first.

'It's Angus McTavish.' Alasdair responded to the look that must have crossed her face. The elderly farmer was well known for calling them out for home visits which could just as easily have been solved with a phone call. 'I don't think he's time-wasting, for once. There's been an accident up the farm, but it's not Angus — it's his grandson Craig.'

'Is it serious?'

'Sounds like it could be, but the air

ambulance is at a multi-car pile-up on the main road from Glenbervie, which is also making the access into Balloch Pass difficult, so it could take a while for the paramedics to arrive by road too. We can get there in less than five minutes.'

'Okay.' Evie swallowed hard. They could be confronted with anything when they got to the farm, from a minor accident to . . . She didn't really want to consider the worst of the possibilities. Following Alasdair out of the cottage at a running pace, she concentrated on her breathing. What was it her mother had always said? Prepare for the worst, hope for the best, and take what comes.

* * *

Alasdair brought his four-wheel drive to a screeching halt as he pulled up outside the McTavish farmhouse.

'Ready?'

Evie only nodded in response. If her

voice had come out in a squeak it might have betrayed her fear. The incident on the railway line had all happened so quickly on the day she'd arrived that she hadn't had time to react. This time, though, there'd been the opportunity to mull over every possible scenario; and a farm accident that warranted a request for the air ambulance, involving a young lad, could be as bad as they came. There was a reason she hadn't gone into emergency medicine, and dealing with situations like this was it.

Several vehicles pulled in behind Alasdair, and it seemed like word had got out to the town.

'He's down by the hay barn!' A near-hysterical middle-aged woman had run up the farm track towards them. 'Please Dr. James, he's pinned under the tractor and he's gone the most awful colour.'

'We're here now, Jessie. It's going to be okay.' If Alasdair doubted the truth of his words, he didn't show it. Whether it helped the woman to feel less panicky or not, Evie didn't know, but it worked for her.

Running behind Alasdair, she was aware of footsteps following them down the track: half the town seemed to have turned up to see if they could help. Rounding the corner to a muddy paddock next to a barn, she got her first glimpse of the scene. A tractor was lying on its side, although she couldn't see Craig. The vehicle was attached by a chain to another tractor which seemed to be deeply embedded in the mud.

'This is all my fault.' Angus McTavish suddenly appeared from behind the upturned tractor. 'I told Craig to pull the other one out of the mud, but he didn't know to stop when there was too much resistance. I was shouting, but he didn't hear me, and then all of a sudden it just went over with him underneath.'

The tractor was fairly small, probably not strong enough to do the job of pulling the other tractor out in the first place, but that was a good thing now that it was on top of the boy. At least there was some chance that Craig could survive trapped under that.

'Don't worry about that now, Angus.' Evie found her voice, laying a hand on the old man's shoulder as Alasdair rushed past him towards the upturned vehicle. 'We're here now, and we'll do all we can to help Craig.' Unlike Alasdair she couldn't quite bring herself to promise him it would be okay.

'Oh no.' Alasdair spoke the two words under his breath, but following him round to the other side of the tractor, Evie was close enough to hear them. The boy had obviously tried to throw himself clear of the vehicle as it tipped, but he was trapped with one leg almost invisible under the weight of the tractor, save for the very top of his thigh. There was a pool of red colouring the mud around it, which could only be one thing.

Evie felt for a pulse as she knelt down beside the boy. It was rapid, but still quite strong.

'Craig, it's Evie Daniels. Dr. James

and I are here to help you.' She put her face close to the boy's as she spoke. His breathing was shallower than she wanted, and he didn't respond at all when she spoke to him. 'He's going to need the oxygen.'

Evie moved towards Alasdair, who handed her the portable canister of oxygen from his kit. Thank goodness he'd been on call and had everything they needed in his car. As a doctor in a rural area, he carried far more kit than the average GP.

'I'll give him some morphine; if he comes round, we're going to need to keep him calm.' Alasdair administered the injection as Evie positioned the oxygen mask. They worked swiftly, without the need to exchange many words. The woman who'd met them on the driveway, who Evie assumed must be the boy's mum, was openly sobbing now.

'We can get the tractor off him, Doc, it's what we came up for,' one of the men who had followed them up to the farm shouted across the paddock. Thankfully, the crowd that had seemed to gather from nowhere were keeping a respectful distance.

'How long has he been under the tractor?' Alasdair spoke directly to Angus.

'About fifteen minutes.'

'Do you think we should lift it off?' Alasdair turned to Evie and then gestured towards the dark red pool staining the ground beneath Craig's trapped thigh.

'It looks like he's bled quite badly, and if it's the tractor that's keeping the pressure on it, he could bleed out if we suddenly lift it off — or we could risk crush syndrome — so we need to decide quickly.' Evie had done a stint in the accident and emergency department during her training, but she'd never had to deal with anything as front-line as this. The paramedics and air ambulance had always been burdened with this sort of decision and, as a junior doctor, she'd just done what she was told when the patients arrived at hospital. Now it was down to her and Alasdair in a life-or-death situation.

'I know, but looking at the colour of him, I don't think we can afford to leave it either.' Alasdair kept his tone low, as aware as Evie was that the boy's family were standing only feet away from them.

'I think we've got to tourniquet his leg and get the vehicle off.' Evie glanced towards where the boy's mum was kneeling in the mud, holding his hand. She was telling him she loved him and that they'd get him out, but he wasn't responding. No mother should have to go through that. 'I know there's a risk of ischemia and other complications with a tourniquet, but it's got to be our best shot to stop the bleeding and prevent toxins flooding the body when we lift the tractor off.'

'Let's do it.' Alasdair reached into his bag and took out a blue band with a white buckle attached. Evie checked the boy's pulse again; it was fluctuating, so every second counted.

Clawing at the mud around the boy's leg with his bare hands, Alasdair made a groove to pull the tourniquet through. Evie held her breath as he positioned the strap in the exposed part of Craig's thigh and tightened the buckle. There was no real way of knowing whether it was in the right position on not when they couldn't see where the injury was.

'How's his pulse?' Alasdair looked across at Evie, who nodded her head. The speed had seemed to steady a bit with the application of the tourniquet and the morphine kicking into his system. The boy's mother was still kneeling on the other side of him, stroking his hair which was matted with mud.

'Are we going to try to lift this now?' She looked at the tractor. It had been smaller than she'd expected, but all the same it suddenly seemed like a mammoth task.

'They are.' Alasdair nodded his head to where around twenty of the locals were standing, looking ready to be called into action at any moment. 'We need to rope the tractor up, though; there can't be any risk of it slipping once they start to lift it. Ideally we need to get it right off him, in case he's got spinal or neck injuries too, but if they can only lift it up enough for us to slide him out, we're going to have to go for it.'

'Absolutely.' As before, it was a question of weighing up two risks and picking the lesser of them. It wasn't an easy choice, but if it was her life in the balance, Evie would absolutely trust Alasdair to do the right thing. Craig didn't have the option of being part of the decision, so they had to trust their instincts.

'Right, lads; I need you to lift the tractor up for us now, but I want it roped up.' Alasdair shouted the command at the group of men waiting to spring into action. 'Angus, have you got some rope?'

'There's plenty of it in the barn.' The

elderly farmer seemed to shake himself back to life, his face almost as pale as that of his grandson trapped beneath the tractor. He started to half hobble and half run in the direction of the barn.

'Leave it Angus, stay with the boy, I'll get the rope.' One of the men shouted across and turned to sprint towards the barn. Within seconds, a group of them were down by the tractor, one of them carrying a large length of rope.

Alasdair was still speaking in a calm, authoritative tone, telling the men exactly how he wanted the tractor roped up and the direction he wanted it pulled. All the time, Evie was checking the boy's pulse and intermittently reaching out to squeeze his mother's hand. Things were moving fast now, but it must have seemed an eternity for the poor woman, watching her son lie helpless in the mud as everyone worked around him.

'On the count of three, lift.' Alasdair shouted the instruction and never once moved from his position by the tourniquet. If the tractor fell as they lifted it, he was in just as much danger as Craig. Evie wanted to tell him to be careful, but she knew he'd put his patient first whatever the cost to him. It was one of the things that drew her to him. Pushing the thought out of her head, she held her breath as Alasdair shouted out his next instruction. 'One, two, three, lift!'

A terrific squelching sound signified success as the tractor was pulled free of the mud bath it had landed in.

A jet of wet mud shot up, spraying across the casualty and hitting Evie in the face. Wiping it off with the back of her hand, she noticed Craig's eyes flicker for a second and then close again. His pulse was rapid now.

'He's got a compound fracture.' As Alasdair spoke, Evie looked down towards the boy's injured leg. The fractured bone jutted out from a rip in his jeans, a few inches below where Alasdair had applied the tourniquet.

'I'll get the antibiotics.' The conditions for an open fracture could hardly have been worse. Evie had taken in the state of the field, which looked as though it was probably used to graze cattle for most of the time, and there'd obviously been slurry-spreading at some point. The risk of infection couldn't have been higher. 'Do you know if he's had a tetanus injection in the last five years?' She turned towards his mother as she spoke.

'I can't remember, I . . . '

'Don't worry, we'll give him a booster, we just need to prevent any infection getting into the wound.'

Evie set up the IV antibiotics in the boy's arm, giving his mother the bag of fluid to hold, as she administered a tetanus injection — all the while aware of Alasdair assessing the severity of the injury. She couldn't help hoping it was something they could leave until the ambulance arrived.

'Can you see if you can feel a pulse in his ankle?' Alasdair's expression had changed suddenly and Evie knew what he was going to say next, before he said it. 'I think there's an issue with the distal circulation.'

Evie scrambled across the mud to the other side of Alasdair. Peeling back the boy's sock slightly, the colour of his foot told her all she needed to know before she even felt for a pulse.

'We're going to have to realign it rather than splint it, aren't we?' There was a good chance he'd end up losing the leg altogether if they didn't act now.

'Yes.' Alasdair touched her hand for the briefest of moments. 'We can do this.'

'What do you want me to do?'

'If you can keep monitoring the colour and circulation, I'll try to realign it. Then we can get it splinted.'

Evie nodded. She had the better end of the deal, but it didn't stop her hoping they'd hear the ambulance siren at any second and be let off the hook. Alasdair would no doubt finish the job either way, but Evie promised herself she'd never moan about an epidemic of chicken pox or a rush of patients with colds again.

Alasdair straddled the boy's leg, stabilising it above and below the injury site, and began to apply gentle traction towards Evie's position at his ankle. She looked up towards Craig, whose eyes were still firmly shut. That was one small mercy, at least; it would have been agonising for him were he awake.

'That's it.' Alasdair turned to her as he managed to move the leg back into the right anatomical position. 'How's the colour?'

'It's looking less grey already.' Evie managed a smile; it was like a small miracle as the colour in the boy's lower leg began to return to normal. 'I've got a pulse at the ankle too.'

'Oh, thank heavens for that!' His mother almost screamed in relief.

'Let's get this leg splinted.' At the very moment Alasdair spoke, the wail of a siren could be heard approaching from the glen below them.

Craig's eyes flickered again, and he moaned loudly as they finally shot open and he pulled the oxygen mask off his face. 'My leg. I turned the tractor over. Granddad's going to kill me. I haven't finished my coursework either, Mum.' All the words came rushing out at once and he cried out again as he tried to lift his head.

'Stay still for a bit longer, Craig. We're just going to splint your leg, and then the paramedics will get you to hospital. The tractor's fine, and I'm sure your mum doesn't mind about the homework; do you, Jessie?' Alasdair was smiling now, relief tangible amongst the crowd of people still watching the drama unfold too.

'Not in a million years.' Jessie kissed her son's forehead. 'Just you lie still, lad, and let these brilliant people finish their work.'

By the time Alasdair and Evie had fitted the temporary splint to his leg, the paramedics were in the field. There was a swift exchange regarding the treatment and drugs that had been administered before they moved him onto the stretcher.

'I can never thank you enough.' The boy's mum hugged Evie and Alasdair in turn. 'You saved my son's leg, and probably his life too. If there's ever anything I can do for you, just say the word.'

'The lads who lifted the tractor off are just as much to thank as we are. Thanks lads!' Alasdair finally managed to disentangle himself from Craig's mum and shouted the thankyou up to the crowd, who gave a small cheer in response. 'I think that and the muddiness of the field were probably the biggest factors. Thank goodness it was soft enough to cushion his leg a bit, which must have lessened the injury. He's lost a bit of blood, but I'm sure they'll get him sorted out at the hospital. He's going to be okay.'

'Because of you two.' His mother wasn't going to be put off easily.

'We were just doing our job.' Evie

squeezed her hand again as she spoke. 'Now you need to get into the ambulance with him and get to the hospital.'

'Say whatever you like, hen, but the two of you more than did your job today. You saved my whole world.' Jessie gave her one final hug before turning and running after the paramedics. 'I'll call Dr. James from the hospital as soon as there's more news.'

'Congratulations, Dr. Daniels, I think that's the third miracle you've performed in the short time you arrived in Balloch Pass.' Alasdair's dark eyes clouded with so much tenderness she wanted to kiss him there and then, even in front of the crowd of locals who showed no sign yet of dispersing.

'I think it had far less to do with me than it did with you.'

'We're a team, aren't we?' Alasdair's eyes crinkled in the corners. 'You look like you've been into battle.'

'Well, I won't need to bother with a mud pack for a while, that's for sure.'

She reached up to touch the mud that had splattered on to her face, which was now drying out.

'You don't need to bother with any beauty treatments. You couldn't look any better.'

'Even covered in mud like this?'

'Even like that.' He moved his head towards hers and she was sure he was about to kiss her again, but then there was another roar of approval from the crowd, and his head shot up in response. 'Shall we finish this later?'

'I think that would be a fantastic idea.' Evie turned to see a paramedic striding back towards them across the field.

'I know it's an imposition, but would one of you mind coming with us to the hospital? I think it would be really useful if you could brief the orthopaedic surgeons personally about exactly what happened.'

'I'll go.' The disappointment in Alasdair's voice echoed Evie's emotions. Would they ever get a chance to be together? He handed her his keys. 'Take my car back to the cottage, and I'll call you when I know what's going on.'

'I'll see you later, then.' She tried and failed to keep the regret out of her voice.

'It's a promise.' With that, Alasdair was gone, and she just hoped it was one more promise he could live up to. But as she watched the flashing lights of the ambulance disappear into the glen below them, she couldn't help wishing that for once they could stop being doctors first.

7

Alasdair was beginning to wonder if the universe was trying to tell him something. He'd been as quick as he could at the hospital, and Angus McTavish, who'd followed the ambulance in his pick-up truck, had offered to give him a lift home, having established that his grandson Craig was definitely okay and that there was nothing any of them could do until he came out of surgery.

If it hadn't been for his phone ringing as they got out to the car park, he might even have made it back to the Balloch Pass Inn and had the chance to spend some time alone with Evie. The desire to hurl his phone off the car park rooftop was almost overwhelming, but when he saw Josh's name flash up on the screen, there was only one option. He had to answer it.

'I think I'm coming down with

man-flu.' Josh laughed. 'I know a cold can't hold a candle to most of the things you're call out for, but it really seems to be wiping me out this time. The kids are full of excitement because it's Friday night, and I'm just not sure I can live up to their expectations. Rory has got a Lego fort he's desperate to build, and Bronte wants me to go to a tea party for her bears. I think I'm just about up to the latter, but Rory's asking if you can come over and do some building with him later, if you haven't got anything on?'

What was he supposed to do? Tell a little boy who'd lost his parents that he was sorry but he couldn't come over, as there was a woman he couldn't get out of his head waiting from him to turn up? There was no choice in the end. He just hoped Evie would understand.

'Of course, I'll be straight over. I'm just leaving the hospital now, so I'll get Angus to drop me at your place.'

'You're at the hospital? Nothing serious, is it?'

'I'll tell you all about it when I get over there.'

Ending the call, he texted Evie: *I'm so sorry. Everything's okay at the hospital and Craig has gone into surgery, but Josh phoned me on the way out and he's feeling really rough. He needs my help with Bronte and Rory, so I'm going round — but please don't think it's because I don't want to spend time with you. Alasdair.*

He hesitated before he sent the message. Maybe the universe was trying to tell him something for a reason. Evie was determined not to stay in Balloch Pass, which had something to do with a promise to her mother, but he still wasn't sure why she wouldn't even consider it. He suspected there was more to the story than she'd told him, a deeper reason for her not wanting to settle down — maybe even a broken heart lying at the root of it all. It just made her all the more intriguing. Not that he'd been entirely honest about why Balloch Pass was the *one and only* place for him, whether he wanted it to be or not. Telling her about his promise to Pete and Isabella, to raise Bronte and Rory in the town where they'd been born, would have made it all real. He was under no illusion that Josh would by some miracle hold out on restarting his career until the children reached adulthood, but somehow he just couldn't say it out loud in case that made it real. How could he ever how to live up to his promise and parent the children any-where near as well as Peter and Isabella had?

If he told Evie about Josh's hopes of moving to the Philippines, there was a risk that someone else might find out too and, even worse than that, it could get back to Rory or Bronte from another child in the playground. Josh had been honest from the start that he wouldn't be able to settle down in Balloch Pass forever, but he was adamant that the children shouldn't be told anything until there were some definite plans in place. He and Alasdair had discussed it and agreed that, although it would come as a shock to the children when the end came, the trade-off of them worrying about it long before they needed to was worth it. Since losing their parents, the continuity of their everyday lives had helped Bronte and Rory to get through, so staying at the local school and in the only house they'd ever known was top of the priority list. Josh had considered taking them with him when he found the right job, but they'd both known it had never really been an option. Alasdair was more tied to Balloch Pass than he'd ever been, so if he couldn't convince Evie to stay, then he had to accept the fact that whatever they had would be fleeting. Maybe losing her would be worse in the long run, but this was one attraction he'd lost all desire to fight back at the cottage. Josh was right after all that sometimes life needed to be lived for the moment — the future would have its turn and there was nothing you could do about that.

His phone pinged, announcing the arrival of a text: *Don't give it another thought. Of course you've got to help Josh with the children, I hope he's okay. Good news about Craig, it was touch and go there for a bit, wasn't it? I just wanted to say that I don't think I've ever enjoyed working with a colleague as much as I do with you. Thanks again for letting me have the cottage, and maybe I can sort out picking up the key when you have a moment? Sorry I won't get to see you this evening, but some things are more important than that. xx*

Alasdair took a deep breath and hit the reply button as Angus McTavish bounced out of a pothole at considerable speed.

I really like working with you too, and that's not the only thing I like about you. Are you free to meet up tomorrow? I could give you the key then and maybe we could have lunch together too? x

This time he added the kiss he'd give

almost anything to deliver in person. Anything except let the children down.

Another message arrived: *Meeting up would be great, but do you think Josh will be able to manage with the children on his own if he's still feeling awful tomorrow? Maybe we could take them out for the day, to the zoo or something. The forecast looks good. xx*

A big part of him liked her even more for putting the children first, even though it meant they still wouldn't get the chance to be alone. They were part of a countywide out of hours' service that covered the weekends and evenings on a rota basis, so neither of them were on call. But he hadn't exactly factored a trip to the zoo into their plans. Still, if Josh was calling him for help, then he was really suffering — maybe even with a full-blown case of the flu, despite his bravado on the phone. In all likelihood, the children would need entertaining for the whole weekend. Either way, he'd rather have Evie's company than not, so making plans seemed like a good idea.

After all, Josh had been the one to tell him not to cut the children off from Evie, so why shouldn't they have a day out together? The more he thought about it, the more he liked the idea. He tapped at his phone.

If you're sure you don't mind, that would be great. The kids will love it. Would you be okay to come over to their place at about eleven in the morning, as you've still got my car? Thanks for being so wonderful, by the way. x

He smiled when, barely two minutes later, his phone beeped again.

It's a small sacrifice to make to spend the day with my favourite doctor. Don't stay up too late playing Monopoly with the kids. See you in the morning. xx

Looking across as Angus McTavish as they finally pulled up outside Josh's place, the old man was smiling.

'I told my daughter there was something going on between you and Doc Daniels.' He grinned again, revealing just how many teeth he'd lost over the years.

'No wonder we were hitting potholes like that — you should keep your eyes on the road instead of trying to read other people's texts!'

'Aye, you're right; and don't worry, your secret's safe with me. She's a bonny wee thing, though. Half your luck, Doc!'

'Thanks for the lift, Angus, and let me know if there's any news about Craig, won't you?' It was easier to ignore his remarks than to get into a conversation about Evie. If he tried to deny there was anything going on between them, he was sure his face would give the game away in an instant.

'Aye, I will. Thanks to you and Doc Daniels, I reckon he'll be back out on the farm by Christmas.' The old man didn't miss the look that must have crossed Alasdair's face. 'Don't worry, we'll be much more cautious in the future. Don't think I don't know just how much you did for him. I'll never take any risks with the lad again.'

'That's good to hear. Night, Angus.'

Alasdair got out of the pick-up truck and shut the door behind him. Bracing himself, he walked up the driveway to the house, suddenly hoping that building a Lego fort would be the most difficult part of the evening ahead. Josh had been waiting on hearing about the job in the Philippines ever since he'd got back from his week down in London. If the news was in, everything might be about to change much sooner than either of them had bargained on.

★   ★   ★

Evie set off for Rory and Bronte's house just before eleven o'clock, stopping at the bakery on the way to pick up some still-hot sausage rolls and iced buns, so they could have a little picnic when they arrived. Maggie, her landlady, had agreed to lend her a couple of flasks, so she'd made up hot chocolate for the children and tea for herself and Alasdair. Although the days were shortening and it was getting cooler on the whole, she'd woken to one of those bright autumn mornings when everything seems right with the world. The series of horse chestnut trees that flanked the avenue leading up to the house defined the season, a riot of gold and orange forming a stunning canopy that offered a last glorious display before the leaves fell to the ground.

She just hoped Alasdair's evening had been okay. She'd texted to double-check that the trip to the zoo was still on, and he'd replied to say that the children were looking forward to it almost as much as him. It was funny how much she was anticipating it too, since the idea had popped into her head. She hadn't been herself in years, but trips to London Zoo had been a regular occurrence for her and her mother when she'd been younger. They'd pretend they were explorers in the deepest South American jungle, or trekking through Africa looking for treasure. Her mother had always had the knack of bringing the ordinary to life, making everything they did together exciting, and she'd loved nothing better than to be out in the fresh air. She might have raised Evie alone, but her daughter had never wanted a second parent: her mother had given her an idyllic childhood filled with adventure, despite not actually being able to afford to take her to any of the places they imagined themselves being. It had been more than enough for Evie, though, and the memories would stay with her forever. She'd seen a leaflet for the zoo in the wooden display rack in the porch of the hotel and the thought of taking the children there with Alasdair had made her smile. Unless she'd read him very wrong, he'd be the sort of fun godfather who'd be more than willing to pretend they were on some sort of expedition though the jungle when they walked through the open lemur enclosure that was one of the zoo's biggest selling points.

The children must have been watching at the window for her to arrive, and they shot out of the front door with Alasdair in hot pursuit. She slid across into the passenger seat as Rory and Bronte ran down the path.

'Hello Evie, I've lost my first tooth.' Bronte jumped straight into the back of Alasdair's car and pulled at the corners of her mouth to reveal the gap in her teeth. 'I put it under my pillow last night and the tooth fairy gave me five pounds! She's never given Rory that much before.'

'That's because ... ' Rory, who joined his sister in the back seat, started to speak, but then looked at Evie — who raised her eyebrows. Having never had a sibling, she found it fascinating to watch the way brothers and sisters interacted, and she'd been sure Rory was about to fill Bronte in on exactly who'd played the role of the tooth fairy the night before. 'It's because the price of teeth must have gone up since I lost my last one.'

Evie gave Rory a quick thumbs-up as Alasdair got into the driver's seat. There was a smile playing around his mouth.

'It's all right; I *have* changed after all that business up at the farm yesterday. I keep some clothes at Josh's now, just in case.'

'Was everything okay last night?'

'I think Josh has picked up a virus, but thankfully it doesn't seem to be contagious, and these two definitely need to run off a bit of steam. Even seventeen games of Frustration last night didn't quite take the edge off their energy.' Alasdair laughed, and she knew she'd been right. He was definitely the sort of godfather who'd embrace the whole jungle expedition experience. Not for the first time, she cursed the timing of having met him so soon. If she'd done even a few of the things she'd planned to by now, maybe she'd have been ready to stay in Balloch Pass. The town was beautiful, and she loved the variety of work that came as a GP working in a rural community: the incident at the farm the day before was something she'd never have got the chance to be involved in had she stayed in London. But Alasdair was undoubtedly the biggest draw. She couldn't remember ever been so attracted to someone — though it went beyond that. He was so caring, so strong for everyone who needed him, she felt she could lean against his chest and stay there forever. The fact she'd found the one person who could threaten her promise to her mother so soon seemed like the worst sort of irony.

'Let's go, then. I've already put the postcode into the satnav.' Evie turned round and smiled at the children. 'Who's ready for an adventure?'

'Me!' They both shouted the response and Alasdair laughed again.

'I hope you brought some ear defenders with you!'

'No, just a picnic of sausage rolls, iced buns, tea and hot chocolate.'

'You're just about perfect, Evie Daniels.' Alasdair glanced in her direction, the longing she felt reflected in his face.

*   *   *

'This was such a brilliant idea.' Alasdair took her hand in his as they struggled to keep up with Evie and Rory, who were running along the path towards the gorilla house. He clearly didn't care who saw them holding hands, or if the resulting gossip swept through Balloch Pass.

'Are you sure you want this?' She looked up at him, certain now that she wanted more than friendship, even though it might cost her heart.

'Some things are worth the risk.' It was almost as if he'd read her mind and taken the very next words out of her mouth. 'We both know where we stand. You can't stay, and I can't go because of . . . the surgery. Let's not worry about the future until we need to, though. Deal?'

'Deal.' It was easier said than done, and if she'd made the promise to anyone but her mother, she wouldn't have needed any persuasion to stay. But there were some bonds even death couldn't break.

'I'm trying to take a leaf out of their book.' Alasdair looked towards where

Bronte and Rory had skidded to a halt outside a huge sheet of glass at the front of the gorilla house.

'They seem so happy, despite everything.'

'The funny thing is, I think they really are. Maybe it was because Pete and Isabella did such a fantastic job with them before the accident that it's just carried them through. They were an amazing couple, Evie; I wish you'd had the chance to know them.'

'Me too.' Evie wished Alasdair and her mother had met too. They would have got along, she was sure of it, but it hurt to know that she could fall in love and never be able to tell her mum about the wonderful man she'd met. Was she in love with him? It certainly felt like it. A broken engagement in the days after her mother died had made her doubt her judgment, though. She thought she'd loved David and that he'd loved her — but he'd let her down so badly and she'd seen him for what he really was. Her mother had never been convinced he was right for Evie, and it turned out that mothers really did know best sometimes. Now she had to rely on her own judgement, and the overwhelming feeling that her mother would have liked Alasdair. A lot.

'Look, that gorilla's doing the other one's hair!' Bronte squealed with delight as Evie and Alasdair caught up with them outside the gorilla house. It was a conservation zoo, with a focus on rescuing animals and a breeding programme to support endangered species. The leaflet had said the gorilla house was world-renowned for the work it was doing, and it was amazing to get up close with the animals. Bronte's little face said it all.

'My mum loved gorillas.' Rory's voice was a stark contrast to his sister's excitement and Alasdair crouched down to the boy's level.

'I know she did.' He put an arm around Rory, who leant into him for just the briefest of moments before straightening himself up again.

'We used to watch programmes about them on TV together, and she said she'd take me to see them in the wild one day.' Rory sniffed, and Evie longed to reach out and envelope him in a hug, but she could tell he was struggling to keep it all together.

'She didn't mean to break her promise, Rory, you know that.' Alasdair kept his arm firmly around the boy's shoulder, and a little piece of Evie's heart broke for the children. They needed adventure and escape more than anyone.

'She was always saying *one day*, to lots of places she was going to take us, but she never got round to it.' Rory's voice caught on the words. 'She should have done it while she had the chance.'

'You could still do all those things, Rory.' Evie spoke quietly, struggling to keep her own emotions in check at the unfairness of it all. 'My mum had a book of all the places she wanted to visit, but she didn't get a chance to go to any of them before she died, so I promised I'd see them for her.' It

173

sounded so simple when she said it out loud, but she was already stumbling at the first hurdle.

'I've got a One Day box too!' Rory was suddenly smiling. 'I cut out pictures and drew some too of the all the places that Mum and Dad were going to take me; it's all in a tin box under my bed. Maybe me, Uncle Josh and Bronte could start going to some of the places, when he gets better?'

'I'd love to see your One Day box sometime.' Evie swallowed against the huge lump lodged in her throat.

'Okay. Will you show me your book too? I could get some ideas then of where else we could go.' Rory's eight-year-old enthusiasm was successfully pushing his grief to one side again.

'I'd love to show you, except that the book disappeared just before I came up to Scotland.' Evie forced a smile, tapping lightly on the side of her head. 'But I've stored all the things in the book up here, and I know where Mum wanted to go.'

Bronte suddenly let out an ear-piercing scream as one of the silverback gorillas banged his fist on the glass in front of them.

'Can we go to a different part of the jungle now?' She clung onto Evie's hand as if her life depended on it. She was obviously scared, but still keen to continue their explorer game.

'How about the elephants?'

'Yes, let's go there!' Her confidence restored, Bronte let go of Evie's hand and began to skip after Rory, who picked up the park map and was expertly directing them to the elephant paddock within seconds.

'I'm so sorry, I shouldn't have mentioned my mother's book and given Rory the idea he could visit all the places his mum and dad promised to take him.' Evie waited until the children were out of earshot before she spoke.

'You made him happy, and that gave him hope. We all need a bit of that sometimes, and maybe Josh will be able to sort some of those things out for him.' Alasdair stopped and put his hands on her shoulders, turning her to face him. 'You didn't do anything wrong.'

'I just wish there was something more I could do for them.'

'I know.' He whispered the words into her hair as he pulled her towards him and she had that feeling again, as if she could stay happily stay there forever.

'Uncle Alasdair, kissing is gross.' Rory was suddenly standing in front of them again, having doubled back when they weren't following as instructed.

'We weren't kissing, Rory.' Alasdair's protests fell flat as the young boy shook his head.

'If you say so, but we're never going to finish this expedition if you two keep messing about.' He suddenly sounded about forty years old, and neither Alasdair or Evie could stop themselves from laughing.

'Do you know what? You sounded just like your Uncle Josh.' Alasdair was still smiling as he took hold of Evie's hand again.

'Well, he does say that to me and Bronte quite a lot.' Rory was smiling now too, and Evie's heavy heart lifted.

* * *

They finished the day with the lemur walk that Evie had told the children all about on the journey over. Alasdair was tempted more than once to tell her about his promise to Pete to look after the children when he was gone, and that Josh was thinking of moving on, but he couldn't risk even the slightest chance that one of them might overhear. Yet a big part of him wanted her to understand why he'd been holding back in the same way she had, but for very different reasons. She was so brilliant with the children, but that was a big risk in itself. Whatever Josh said, he couldn't risk the children getting too close an attachment to Evie, only to have her walk out of their lives as well. This living for the moment was a lot more difficult than people made it sound.

'I think that lemur has taken a shine to you.' Evie was laughing as the animal followed Rory about a pace behind and, every time the little boy stopped to look at it, stopped dead in its tracks too.

'It's probably your boy stink.' Bronte spoke with the great authority that five-year-old girls could possess when they knew they were right about something.

'More like he's staying out of the way of your girl stink.' Rory shot her the sort of look that only big brothers could get away with.

'I think he just recognises an explorer when he sees one,' Alasdair intervened, and hoisted Bronte on to his shoulders before she could be upset by the fact that she clearly wasn't as much of an explorer as her brother. 'Lemurs also know that princesses should ride through the jungle; so I'll be your horse, Bronte, okay?'

'Okay, Uncle Alasdair, but make sure you stop if I say whoa!'

'You're great with the kids.' Evie fell into step beside him.

'I was just thinking the same about you.'

'I suppose all this is part of the appeal of Balloch Pass, the long-standing friendships you have here, the sort of place where you might want to raise your own family?' She sounded wistful, and more than ever he wanted to tell her that the decision had already been made for him.

'I haven't really thought about having a family of my own until recently.' He paused, it was true. He'd never felt the kind of connection with anyone that had made him want to go into a *forever* set-up. The family he envisaged now was a ready-made one, just at the point where someone had come into his life who he could have had that connection with. 'What about you, do you want that? A family and a house with a white picket fence?'

'I'm not so bothered about the fence!' She laughed, and the sound made him want to take her face in his hands and kiss her again. 'But I definitely want children. Eventually.'

'Whoa, Uncle Alasdair, you can let me down now.' Bronte pulled on his ears as if they were reins, and he lifted her off his shoulders. 'I'm going to tell the lemur that's following Rory how horrid he is sometimes. Then he might follow me instead.'

'Okay, darling; but don't get too close to the animals, alright?' Alasdair smiled as Bronte nodded in response and trotted off after Rory, he and Evie following on behind. 'Tell me a bit more about the promise you made your mum.'

'She had this bucket list book, where she'd listed all the places she didn't get a chance to go to before she got ill. She did everything for me when I was a child, working to support us both, but still making sure I never came home to an empty house. She had a part-time job at the local school in the daytime, so we didn't have much money. My dad was never on the scene, and she did some bookkeeping in the evening to pay for treats, days out to the zoo like this, but we never had the sort of money that stretched to foreign holidays. I never minded as a child, because she could make a trip to the park something magical, she just had this way about her. It's another thing I'm really sad about, that my children won't get to have her around as a grandma. She'd have been amazing.'

'She sounds it.' Alasdair hesitated, wanting to tell Evie that she'd inherited her mother's ability to make a day out into an adventure, but there were still some boundaries he needed to maintain. 'So is that what you're doing, visiting the places on her list?'

'At least some of them.' Evie frowned. 'When I left London, I left pretty quickly. I was supposed to be getting married before Mum got ill, but David couldn't cope with my grief when she was diagnosed, and he all but disappeared in the weeks that led up to her death, preferring the company of other women. Mum could see he was a carbon copy of my dad; there for the good times, but not someone who could cope with any sort of responsibility. She begged me not to settle for a life with someone like that; she wanted me to have it all, to see the places she never saw. She'd started planning a trip round the world when I first went to university. A couple of years ago, she got a job as an accounts manager for a high-end car dealership in London, and she was earning really good money for the first time in her life, saving to see the world. But in the end, there wasn't enough time left for her to do it.'

'No wonder you wanted to get away from London after all of that.' Alasdair took her hand in his again, looking up to see both children happily leaning against the fence and watching three of the lemurs chase each other along the ropes strung above their heads, their earlier spat clearly forgotten.

'I did. I couldn't bear to be around David when he started to act as if everything should go back to normal as soon as Mum died. So I gave notice for my job and just packed everything up and left. I was going to head straight overseas, but it would have taken too long to plan, so the Scottish Highlands seemed like the next best thing. I could have sworn I'd packed Mum's book with the bucket list in it, only it wasn't in my things when I got here. I couldn't bear to look at it after she died, so I was saving it until I felt strong enough — only now I can't because it's gone. I messaged David to ask him to send it up to me, but he said he couldn't find it amongst the stuff I'd left behind either. So, I don't have the list, but I know the places she talked about the most in the weeks that led up to her death. So that's what I'm doing, seeing those places for mum and living up to my promise not to settle down anywhere until I have.'

'I can't help wishing you'd found

Balloch Pass a bit later on your travels.'

'Me too.' Evie turned to look at him, naked regret in her eyes. 'But she also told me to make the most of every day and I think that's what we're doing, isn't it?'

'I think so.' In truth, Alasdair wasn't sure, but despite his doubts he wanted to be with Evie while he could. He was having to get quite good at compart-mentalising the future, the loss of Pete and Isabella, and eventually Evie, was beyond his control.

★ ★ ★

'I wish we could have a pet lemur.' Rory was clutching the stuffed toy lemur Evie had bought him at the zoo's shop on the way out. Bronte had a gorilla that was almost as big as her, and which she was carrying on her shoulders in the same way Alasdair had carried her earlier.

'Or a dog or a kitten.' Bronte stuck out her bottom lip. 'But Uncle Josh said we have to wait.'

'He said he'd think about it soon, Bronte, you know that.' Rory uncharacteristically took his sister's hand, and Evie felt the lump forming in her throat again.

'You'll get a dog *and* a kitten one day, I promise.' Alasdair kept his voice level, despite both children looking at him beseechingly.

'Will you get them for us for Christmas, Uncle Alasdair?' Bronte's eyes were round with excitement.

'Maybe not for Christmas, but definitely one day.'

'I'll put that in my One Day box too, then.' Rory paused. 'Only don't make it too long.'

'It won't be long.'

'How about we all go back to the hotel and have some tea and cake?' Evie sensed the need to change the subject.

'That's a great idea! And then we can help Evie move her things into the cottage.' Alasdair smiled as the children screwed up their faces at the prospect of doing what sounded distinctly like chores. 'And then maybe after that we can order a Chinese?'

'Yay!' Bronte squealed with delight.

'Can we have fortune cookies?' Rory nodded his toy lemur's head, as if the monkey was making the request.

'I think that's a given.' Alasdair took Evie's hand again as they made their way back to his car, and she had to bite her lip to stop the threatened tears; it wasn't just Alasdair she was going to miss when she left Balloch Pass.

★ ★ ★

'You're looking a lot better than you did this morning.' Alasdair found Josh sitting at the kitchen table, busy on his laptop when he finally took the children home. They'd rushed off upstairs to find homes for their new soft toys, and Rory wanted to put the motto he'd found in his fortune cookie into his One Day box. It had prophesised that Rory would achieve great things and see the world, and he hadn't been able to keep the smile off his face from the moment he'd opened it.

'I feel much better.' Josh looked almost embarrassed. 'But I think it might also have something to do with the email I got just after you left this morning.'

'They've offered you the job in the Philippines?'

'Not quite yet. They're now down to a shortlist of two, and they want me to fly out on Monday for some more meetings and to see the site where I'd be based.' Josh screwed up his face. 'Do you think I'm completely selfish to want this so much?'

'We've talked about this, Josh. The kids' home is here, but yours isn't, so it makes sense for me to take over.'

'Just because something makes sense, it doesn't necessarily make it easy, does it?' Josh still looked grim-faced and it was obvious he was wrestling with his conscience. But Josh would only end up resenting his role as stand-in parent, and that was the last thing Alasdair wanted the children to feel — as if they were a burden no-one wanted.

'It was never going to be easy for either of us to try and do Pete and Isabella's jobs, but we'll get by — and no-one said you going away has to be forever.'

'True. And I might not even get the job.'

'I think we both know you will.' Alasdair patted him on the back. 'And I genuinely hope you do. I'm as ready as I'll ever be to take this on.'

'Well, you're much more like to provide a mother figure for the kids than me, anyway. I've never been the settling-down type.' Josh laughed. 'I know she's not planning on sticking around forever, but if you end up with someone like Evie, the kids will have the benefit of that too.'

'I wouldn't bank on that.' Alasdair wished it were that easy, but he was starting to realise that there wasn't anyone else like Evie — at least, not for him.

8

'Look who's in the paper!' Susie, the surgery's receptionist, was waving a copy of the local paper in the air the moment Evie arrived at work on Monday. Alasdair, who was standing in front of the reception desk, looked less than impressed by Susie's enthusiasm.

'I think Angus McTavish wanted to find a way of thanking us, and it seems he thought a double-page spread in the *West Highlands Weekly* was just the thing.' Alasdair shook his head.

'It's a great article: there's even a picture of the two of you in the thick of the action that someone must have taken on their mobile phone. And they've used your pictures from the surgery website.' Susie was beaming with pride.

'Great.' Evie was about as enthusiastic as Alasdair looked. She didn't really want this sort of attention — and, as for her picture on the website, she'd been like a rabbit in the headlights the day it had been taken, not at all certain she'd made the right decision to up sticks and move to Scotland.

'Can I have a word before we start the team meeting?' Alasdair's eyes met hers as he spoke and there was that instant reaction in her body again, as if it was somehow recognising its other half, a magnetic force between them.

'Absolutely. In your consultation room?'

'I think that would be best.'

Alasdair closed the door behind them once they were in the room. 'I just wanted to say thanks again for this weekend. The kids had a great time with you. So did I. I'm just sorry we didn't get the chance to spend any time alone at all.'

'I loved being with them, they're really great kids.' Evie smiled at the memory. Even though she knew she wanted children, she'd never thought that much before about becoming a parent, what with concentrating on her studies and her career, and then caring for her own mother. But being with Alasdair and the children at the weekend, she'd really understood how wonderful it could be.

'They're both brilliant. Josh has got to go overseas for work for a couple of weeks, so I'm going to be staying there for a bit, to help out with the children, and do all the running around to their after-school clubs. They've got busier schedules than some CEOs!'

'That makes sense.' Evie bit back her disappointment, determined not to give in to the selfish side the desire to be alone with Alasdair brought out in her.

'Isabella's sister Maria and her husband are in the UK for a while, though, and they're coming up on Saturday morning and staying on until Sunday evening. So I wondered, if you didn't have any plans, whether you might want to spend a day up at the lodge with me?'

'The lodge?' It could have been a garden shed for all Evie cared, as long as Alasdair was there.

'It's a log cabin Pete and I bought as the first of our holiday lets. It's a bit up in the wilds, just inside the edge of the forest that starts on the outskirts of Balloch Pass and stretches out from the glen that leads up to Angus McTavish's farm.'

'It sounds wonderful.'

'I know there's no guarantee how long any of this is going to last, but I want to spend time with you.'

'Living for the moment?' She looked up into his face again and he smiled.

'Well, right now, I'm living for the weekend, so I can spend the day with you.'

Just as he was lowering his face towards hers, there was a sharp rap on the consulting room door.

'Are we starting this meeting or not? Only I've got patients to start seeing in twenty minutes.' It was Julia, the practice nurse, who clearly hadn't woken up on the right side of bed.

'Be right with you!' Alasdair frowned. 'It seems like things just keep getting in our way.'

'Not this weekend.' Evie kissed him lightly on the lips. 'And having to wait to get some time alone is half the fun.'

'Is it?' Alasdair raised an eyebrow. 'You could have fooled me.'

Following him out of the room, Evie barely resisted the urge to do a happy dance, already working out in her head how many hours she had to count down until they could spend a whole day together.

* * *

Isabella's sister and her family arrived very late in the evening on the Friday night in the end. They'd brought enough food to feed an army, and they were full of affection for the children. Maria's own daughters were in their late teens, and had more than enough energy to keep up with Rory and

Bronte's demands for endless games. When Alasdair set off on the Saturday morning, the four cousins were already out in the garden, bouncing on the trampoline and making enough noise for twenty people. It was great to see them with Isabella's family, renewing the connection to their mum, who'd looked so much like their Aunt Maria. He didn't have to feel guilty about leaving them to spend the day with Evie: they were going to have a wonderful time.

When he arrived outside the cottage to pick her up on Saturday morning, and she opened the door, everything else melted away. She was so beautiful, her blonde hair catching the light as she turned to lock the cottage door, and when she turned back to smile at him, he silently prayed they got there before they ran into another emergency. Neither of them was on call, though; and with Isabella's sister in charge, he'd decided to turn his phone off. Nothing was going to stand in the way of spending some time with Evie this weekend; with the way things were with Josh's plans, there was no way of knowing when they'd get another chance. He wanted to find out more about what made her tick. She was a fantastic doctor, obviously fiercely loyal to her mother's memory and keen to get away from her past, with an ex-fiancé who'd badly let her down when she'd needed him. But he knew from the time they'd spent together, and their weekend with the children, how much she liked to laugh and have fun too. He couldn't help wondering what else there was to Evie, beyond the desire to fulfil her mother's legacy. What was it she *really* wanted from life? He was hoping this might be his chance to find out.

'Good morning,' Evie greeted him as she got into the passenger seat. He couldn't stop himself leaning forward to kiss her, even before he'd replied.

'Sorry, it's just that I've been waiting to do that for over a week now, and you looked so fantastic this morning.'

'I could get used to starting every morning like that.' As she spoke, a blush coloured her cheeks. Was it the kiss that had caused it? Or the hint at longevity in their relationship, which they both knew wasn't on the cards?

'Are you ready for a woodland adventure, then?' Alasdair forced his hands back onto the steering wheel. If he really wanted to get to know Evie better, he'd have to get a bit of control back. Easier said than done when she was sitting less than a foot away from him, looking stunning even in a pair of Levis and sensible walking boots.

'I think I've packed for every eventuality. It must be the Girl Guide in me.'

'You were a Girl Guide?'

'Not just that; I helped out with the Brownie pack when I was in the sixth form, and got as high up as being a Tawny Owl.' She laughed at the look that must have crossed his face. 'Alright, I know it makes me sound like a complete nerd, but I thought it would look good on my uni application and help me get accepted for a medical degree.'

'It obviously did the trick.' He turned and smiled at her briefly before pulling onto the road that led out of Balloch Pass to a densely wooded area on the outskirts of the town known as Coille Water. It was named for the river that ran through it, which was wide and fast-flowing in places. It had always been one of Alasdair's favourite spots to spend time, and when the log cabin on the edge of the forest had come up for sale, he'd just had to have it. Thankfully Pete had loved it just as much, and had spent lots of weekends with his family there. Even though it was only a few minutes by car and walkable from his house, if you were in the mood for a hike, he'd always said it could have been a world away.

The short journey passed in easy conversation, and there was more of the gentle teasing they seemed so able to exchange. It was as if the time that they'd known each other could have been measured in years, rather than weeks.

'So, this is it.' He pulled up outside the lodge, a place that never failed to lift his spirits. Not that they needed lifting: Evie was enough to do that all by herself.

'It's amazing!' She turned to him and smiled, throwing her arms around his neck, the heady scent of her perfume making him forget everything else for a moment.

'Not as amazing as you.' She was so easy to compliment; there were so many things he loved about her. 'Shall I show you around inside? We can drop off our bags, and then I thought we could go for a walk before we come back and have some lunch.'

'That sounds wonderful.' Evie threw open the car door as he got out and took the picnic bag off the back seat. She looked like a kid in a sweetshop as she took in the big rope swing hanging from a huge tree outside the cabin, which swung right down across the river for anyone brave — or foolhardy — enough to give it a go.

'I thought you city types hated the countryside, Dr. Daniels.'

'I'd have given anything to spend summers somewhere like this when I was a kid! Like I told you, we didn't have a lot of money, but Mum used to rent a mobile home every summer at Mersea Island in Essex. I used to love being by the seaside, and she made it such an adventure when the tide would cut off the island — albeit temporarily — from the mainland. But we never went anywhere with this feeling of isolation. It's the kind of place where you really could have an adventure.' Their eyes met briefly, and she looked away for a second.

'Come on, let's get the quick guided tour out of the way, then we can start working towards your Wilderness Survival badge. After all, that's what every good Girl Guide wants most, isn't it?'

He laughed as she pretended to push him.

'It's beautiful; the kitchen is like something out of a dream homes magazine. Is it all handmade?' She ran a hand over the reclaimed pine dresser that housed several cupboards and rows of deep shelves, flanking an entire side of the kitchen area. 'I can't believe how much you've been able to cram into the space.'

'I made it myself, to fit the odd shape of the lodge where the roof cuts down.' Alasdair smiled at the look she gave him. Most people were more impressed by his medical background than by his carpentry skills, but as a fellow GP, Evie took a different view. 'It's really not that impressive. As I said at the cottage, I find it a good way to relax, and it's satisfying to stand back and look at something you've made yourself.'

'Well, I think it's really clever. The views from the windows are spectacular too.' She leant towards the large kitchen window, which looked down on the river that had stopped any of the local farms encroaching on the woodland years ago. If it hadn't been there, the lodge would have been walkable from the town in half an hour or so; but, as it was, you had to drive up to the only vehicle crossing almost at the other end of the glen, unless you felt like risking getting very wet by using one of the rough stone crossings. At this time of year, with the water level rising, that definitely wasn't a sensible option. Alasdair liked it that way, though — you could walk for hours in these woods without bumping into a soul.

'Do you fancy seeing a bit more? I thought we could take a walk along the river, then go a bit deeper into the forest — ' He paused for a moment. ' — and, if I get the direction right, we might even end up back on the other side of the lodge at some point.'

'I'm not sure if I'm supposed to be reassured or terrified by that!' She laughed, her blue eyes sparkling in the way that had fired his interest from the first moment they'd met.

'I thought, with you being a Girl Guide, you'd have a compass built into your backpack.'

'I'm sure there's an app for it on my phone, but somehow I don't think we'd get a signal here.'

'I'm banking on it.' He took her face in his hands. 'I really want us to have this time together, so the lack of a phone signal or anyone interrupting us is a big bonus a far as I'm concerned.'

'I want that too.' She pressed her lips against his for the briefest of moments, both of them holding back. 'And getting lost in the woods together is a guaranteed way to get to know someone *really* well!'

* * *

Evie let go of a long breath. This was heaven: a crisp autumn day, walking in stunning surroundings with a man who made her heart beat faster every time she looked at him. He held her hand as they walked along the mossy bank beside the river, clumps of heather adding bursts of colour and the water dashed at speed over the large grey rocks jutting out of the river at various points along the way. There were several waterfalls too, as the ground climbed upwards, curving away from the edge of the town and deeper into the forest.

'It's so beautiful here, I can see why you don't want to leave.' Evie tried to keep the hint of melancholy out of her voice, but wasn't entirely successful.

'It is a fantastic place to live, but it's not just about the surroundings . . . ' He hesitated for a moment, and she was sure he was going to tell her something else, but instead he shook his head. 'I guess it's just home.'

'If I were you, I'd be tempted to move up to the lodge full-time.' Determined not to ruin their time together by talking about a future that inevitably led them in different directions, she changed the subject. 'No constant interruptions or bumping into people whilst you're out in town just wanting you to take a quick look at their suspicious rash!'

'It's tempting, but what if I never came back into town? I'd be forced to make my own clothes out of rabbit skins and grow a three-foot-long beard.'

'If anyone could pull it off, you could.' She loved the easy way they could laugh together; she'd never had that with David. Maybe that's why her mother had never warmed to him, despite her best intentions not to interfere in Evie's love life.

'I'll take that as a compliment, Dr. Daniels.' He pulled her into his arms again and she noticed the grazing of stubble on his cheek. So much more attractive than a three-foot-long beard. He was gorgeous — inside and out. A knot was forming in her stomach, though, and it wasn't just because being with him had this sort of effect on her. How was she supposed to walk away from someone like Alasdair?

'I meant it as a compliment.' She

forced the words out, not saying what she really wanted to say. She wanted to beg him to reconsider leaving Balloch Pass for a while, to take this two-day adventure on the road and see the world together. But that was madness. He had a life in Balloch Pass that he wasn't prepared to give up — he'd made that clear from the start, just as she'd made it clear she had to fulfil her promise to her mother. Only that knowledge didn't stop her longing for something, *anything* to change, so what she was feeling wouldn't have to end.

'I could fall in love with you, you know.' He pushed aside a strand of hair that had blown across her face, looking at her with such intensity she was certain he meant it. She wanted to tell him she felt the same; that, if she was really honest, she'd fallen in love with him a long time before. But saying those things would only hurt them more in the end.

'And I could want you to fall in love with me.' She left it at that, reminding him where they both stood. 'But today's about getting lost, remember. In the woods *and* in the moment.'

'I remember.' He let her go, but kept hold of her hand as they followed the path further into the dense woodland, where the pine trees that seemed to stretch right up to the clouds did their very best to shut the rest of the world out. Just like Evie and Alasdair were doing.

* * *

'I don't think I've ever enjoyed a walk more.' Evie sighed with contentment, her feet curled up under her on one of the sofas that flanked the fireplace, where Alasdair had set a roaring fire.

'Despite the sudden downpour?' He raised an eyebrow. Just as they'd been about to head back towards the lodge, the sky had darkened ominously above the pine trees, and the rain when it came was sudden and heavy, soaking them both to the skin.

'It was all part of the fun, and this is the perfect way to warn up.' Much as she'd enjoyed running through the rain with Alasdair, she'd been shivering by the time they got back to the lodge.

'Maybe a glass of something local will help with that too.' Handing her a tumbler of whiskey, Alasdair smiled.

'Oh, I could get used to this.'

'I brought a couple of steaks up with us, if you've got time to stay for dinner?'

'I didn't think I'd ever eat again after that picnic we had; but now you come to mention it, I could manage a bit more.' She wasn't really bothered about the food, but if it meant she could spend a bit longer with Alasdair, then she'd have even eaten one of those weird Heston Blumenthal dishes — chicken curry ice cream, or something. Luckily they'd had the picnic before the rain set in; and, soaking aside, their time together had been perfect.

'I can't remember enjoying a day like this for . . . ' He looked at her for a long moment. ' . . . actually, I've got nothing more to say. This has been one of my best days ever.'

'Mine too.' She silently cursed the fault in the stars that they'd met before she was ready to settle down, but she shook the thought out of her head.

'I used to think that what Pete and Isabella had was a one-off, and there was no such thing as the perfect person for most people.' He took a seat next to her on the sofa, sticking to coffee as he would be driving them home all too soon. 'But this last week or so, I've been wondering if there really is someone we're meant to be with.'

'I'd like to think so too. When I got engaged to David, I thought we had so much in common and it would make us stable, but all we ever really shared was a medical degree.'

'And is that what you want? Stability?' His dark eyes clouded over.

'All I want now is this moment.' She put down her drink. 'Whatever happens, I'll always be glad I met you. It's opened my eyes to so much.'

He put his hand over hers, and they didn't need any words, they were both making the most of whatever time they had. But if she'd convinced herself that this wasn't love, she knew now that was a lie. She loved being with Alasdair, but more than that she loved *him*. Telling herself anything else was pointless. But one thing she could do was to keep it from him: there was no point in both of them getting hurt by the admission when she eventually moved on.

★ ★ ★

'So have you thought about where you'll go first, after you leave Balloch Pass?' Alasdair broke the silence as the two of them sat in front of the fire after dinner. Part of him had hoped that this time with Evie, getting to know her and maybe finding out she wasn't as perfect as she seemed, would make her leaving easier. An idea that had badly backfired. The more time he spent with her, the stronger his feelings for her became and the harder he found it to think about her leaving, but he had to ask. He had to know how long she was going to be around for, if he was going to stand any chance of successfully living for the moment. Otherwise he'd always be waiting for her to say that now was the time she'd decided to leave.

'Not really.' She turned her face towards him, her eyes reflecting the glow of the fire. 'Before I came here, I had the idea of going to Australia first, taking the furthest point across the world and working my way back, visiting the places Mum most wanted to see. I could picture it all so clearly: releasing a balloon for her on Sydney Harbour Bridge, and hiring a camper van at some point to really see the place. Of course there was always going to be the need to fit some locum work in to pay the bills, but I could imagine myself doing it.'

'Now you don't sound quite so sure.'

'I'm not. Since I came to Balloch

Pass, it's felt like the place I'm supposed to be. And now that we're . . . ' She didn't seem able to finish the sentence, to voice the words that they were together, a blush of colour sweeping across her cheekbones. 'Just lately, I've got the sense of how big a wrench it will be to leave this place. And you.'

'Don't go, then.' He trailed one finger down her face towards her mouth, wanting to stop her saying what she'd say next, even though he knew it was unfair.

'I wish I could stay, you know that. But it doesn't have to be forever, and maybe one day you'll feel like leaving Balloch Pass for a while too, for an adventure of your own.'

'I'm tied to the town in so many ways.'

'I know at the moment, with needing to help Josh out while he settles into taking care of the children, there's no way you could think of leaving.'

'No, and even after that . . . ' He was so close to telling her about his promise to step into Josh's role, but it would have felt like emotional blackmail to mention it. As though he was forcing her to stay, because he *couldn't* leave. 'I just can't ever see myself leaving.'

'We'll just have to keep living for the moment, then.' She lay back against his chest, sounding every bit as unconvinced as he felt. 'And, like I said, right now I'm in no rush to leave.'

'Well, that's one thing we agree on.' It wasn't so bad. After all, the one guarantee anyone really had was the moment they were in. But Alasdair couldn't have known just how few of those moments they'd have left together.

*   *   *

'How were the children yesterday?' Alasdair sat down at the kitchen table where Maria had set out a Sunday morning feast. Her husband Franco had gone off to round up the children.

'Wonderful, as always, but so full of life and on the go constantly!' Maria threw her hands up in the air in a typically Mediterranean gesture, despite her perfect English. 'I know we sometimes wondered if it would be better for them to come and live with us in Italy, but it's clear how happy they are here. I love coming to the house too, and seeing all of Issy and Pete's things. This house has their souls in it, and it's so important for the children to stay here.'

'Has Josh spoken to you?' He couldn't fight the feeling that Maria's words were more than just passing remarks.

'He told me about the possibility of the job overseas, yes.' Maria put another plate of pastries on the table as she spoke. 'But it doesn't matter. It's you the children talk about all the time. I know Josh has been doing his best, but I think Pete and Issy would have wanted you to take care of the children all along.'

'But what if I'm not up to the job?' Alasdair could admit his fears to Maria, and for a moment, when she looked at him, it was like looking straight at Isabella.

'You'll be fine, Ali. Pete and Issy knew you could do it, and I do too.' She crossed the room and kissed him on both cheeks. 'And you know we're only a short plane ride away if you need us.'

'Thank you, Maria, I might just take you up on that.' Alasdair half-heartedly lifted a croissant onto his plate, just hoping that she was right. Bronte and Rory deserved the best, and he'd do whatever it took to make sure they got it. Even if that meant making the ultimate sacrifice and losing the woman he'd only just realised he was in love with.

9

'It's me.' Evie recognised Alasdair's voice immediately, with a little glow of warmth inside because they were already at the stage where they didn't have to say their names. By the time he'd dropped her back at the cottage late on Saturday night, she'd come to the conclusion that she wasn't going to be ready to leave Balloch Pass any time soon. She was planning to wait until their Monday morning meeting at the surgery to tell him she was ready to commit to a year at least. The bucket list wasn't going anywhere, and one thing she knew her mother had wanted for her, above all else, was happiness — something she'd never have if she left Alasdair now. If she was completely honest, part of her still hoped he might rethink his decision to come with her . . . eventually. Anyone with an ounce of decency wouldn't even *think* about leaving whilst Josh clearly still needed so much support with the children, and Alasdair had a whole heap more than an ounce of decency. She'd never ask him to do that anyway; but at some point, their time might come. It was what she was holding on to now, since the day they'd spent together had taken her far beyond settling for the moment. They'd talked for hours — out walking and back at the lodge — and they had a connection she'd never felt before that she couldn't bear the thought of losing.

'I miss you.' If she was supposed to hold back and play it cool, she couldn't help it. It might have been less than thirty-six hours since they'd last seen each other, but even the sound of his voice sent tingles down her spine. She'd never been in love with her ex-fiancé, David; that much was certain now. Thank goodness he'd shown his true colours when he did.

'I miss you too.' Alasdair sounded tired and there was something else in his voice she couldn't quite put her finger on. A hint of regret maybe?

'Is everything okay?'

'Not really.' Alasdair sighed. 'Rory's asthma is playing up, and it looks like he's got the start of a nasty chest infection too; he might even have caught the flu off Josh before he left. I really can't send him to school like this, and with Josh away that would mean sending him to the childminder, but all the poor little soul wants to do is stay tucked up under his duvet at home and have someone to give him a hug when he needs it.'

'Of course he does, and you're the right man for the job. Is there anything I can do?'

'I think it's going to be a while before I can send him back to school, so I've called the agency to get another locum in. They aren't going to get here until tomorrow, so I've asked Susie to rejig all the advance patients for today and keep your appointments to those who really can't wait, so you can cover both our caseloads.'

'Don't worry, if I need to work longer today it's not a problem, and I can show the locum around tomorrow too. Just concentrate on Rory. Susie and I can take care of the rest.'

'What did I do before you came into my life?'

'I don't know what either of us did; but don't worry, I'm here as long as you need me.' It seemed the wrong time to mention her decision to stay for at least a year — she wanted to tell him that face-to-face — but, in that moment, she'd have promised to stay forever if he'd asked her to. Dr. Alasdair James had her heart, and there was no way she'd rather have it.

★ ★ ★

The surgery felt like a different place without Alasdair in it. Thankfully, she was so busy on the Monday fitting in all the appointments that couldn't wait that she barely had time to think, let alone to miss him being around as much as she would otherwise. It was eight o'clock in the evening by the time she got home, having agreed with Susie to extend the surgery's hours for the day until seven. Alasdair had texted to say that he was sorry he hadn't had the chance to call, and that Rory was really suffering with the chest infection and he wanted Alasdair to sit with him all the time. He'd told her he was still missing her, and thanked her again for stepping in to take control of the surgery.

No need to thank me for stuff at the surgery, was Evie's reply message. *I'd do anything for you, I hope you know that. xx*

He texted her back. *I really want to talk to you about things properly, but it's hard at the moment. You'll never know how much difference it makes having you around. x*

She wanted to text him back and tell him about her decision, even to admit how strongly she felt: to actually come right out with it and tell him she loved him. But right now, he needed to focus on Rory; the rest could wait. If she'd known how the arrival of the locum would change everything between her and Alasdair, though, she'd have sent the text. But by then it was all too late.

*   *   *

It felt odd for Evie to be technically in charge at the surgery, when just the week before she'd still felt like the new girl — and a very temporary one at that. Now here she was, about to greet the new locum and attempt to stand in for Alasdair in his absence.

'Morning, Susie.' She called out the greeting as she walked through reception, keen to get things ready for morning surgery before the locum arrived.

'Morning.' Susie's smile could have lit up a dark room. 'The new locum's here already, and he's gorgeous!'

'Gosh, he's early.' Evie silently cursed herself for not checking her emails before she left the cottage. She hadn't even had confirmation from the agency of the locum's identity, let alone his CV. It would be really embarrassing to walk in there and not know his name. 'Have you got his details?'

'All I know is that he's called Dr. Joseph.' Susie giggled. 'I couldn't take in much more than that! I put him in the meeting room until you arrived; he's in there nursing a cup of coffee.'

'Dr. Joseph?' As Evie repeated the name, cold crept up her spine. There were probably hundreds of Dr. Josephs, thousands even . . . It couldn't be him. Thanking Susie, she moved almost robotically towards the meeting room door.

'Evie!' David was up on his feet before she even made it all the way into the room.

'Don't even *try* to tell me this is just a coincidence.' Her voice sounded robotic too, but how were you supposed to react when your ex-fiancé turned up out of the blue?

'Well that wasn't quite the welcome I was hoping for.' David laughed, directing what he passed off as easy charm towards her. It might fool Susie, but Evie could see right through him now.

'I'm surprised you were expecting any sort of welcome. I thought I made it quite clear how I felt.'

'That was the grief talking.' David smiled again, but his eyes were dead, like a shark's.

'It really wasn't.' Evie was getting impatient with him already. She just wanted Alasdair, so working with any locum would have been hard, but working with David was unthinkable. 'And none of this explains how you found me and what you're doing here, working as a locum.'

'I've quit the partnership in London.'

'But all you ever wanted was to set that surgery up.' Evie almost felt the need to pull out a chair and sit down. He'd sidelined her when she'd needed him most because of the focus he'd always had on becoming the founding partner of a surgery before he hit thirty-five. Now here he was, telling her he was working as a locum instead. 'I don't understand.'

'When you left like that, I was angry at first, but then I started to think about why you might have done it and to rethink what I wanted from life.' If she hadn't known him as well as she did, she might have thought he was being sincere.

'And what's that? Being a locum in the Scottish Highlands?'

'Well, if it's good enough for you . . . ' His laugh was hollow this time. 'No, I've lined up a job to go to in Australia. I'm going to be setting up a new surgery in Sydney and I'm just doing a bit of locum work until I leave next month. I'd been trying to track you down since you left, but you'd all but disappeared off the face of the earth. Then I Googled you again one day, and your name came up in an article about that tractor accident.'

'And so — what, the agency just

happened to place you here?'

'I told them I wanted to work in this area of Scotland, although I didn't imagine I'd actually get a posting at your surgery.' His smile was almost sinister now, and Evie shivered in response. 'It was obviously meant to be.'

'David, I don't know what you think is going to happen, but . . . '

'I know what's going to happen.' He cut her off before she could finish the sentence, just like he always had. 'You're going to realise that we made a mistake breaking up and come to Australia with me. I need a good team of doctors there, and you always were one of the best. After all, Australia must have been on your mum's bucket list, so what better place to start?'

'It's not going to happen, David. I've got a life here in Balloch Pass.' She hated him mentioning her mother, the woman he'd just seen as an inconvenience to his own ambitions, even in the months when she was dying.

'Oh, I did wonder. Handsome, isn't he, Dr. James? I thought there might be something between the two of you, from the photos in that article.'

'It's got nothing to do with that.' Evie fought to keep her voice steady, not wanting David to taint what she had with Alasdair too. He was like a poison, his own agenda taking a stranglehold on everything that stood in the way of his ambitions. This wasn't about her, or even what she could offer to his new team at the surgery in Sydney. It was because she'd ended things, and he'd never been able to stand losing.

'Oh, I think it's got everything to do with him. Handsome as he may be, Evie, a backwater like this is never going to be enough for you, and one day the lure of all those promises you made your mum will make you long to leave. You should just come to Sydney with me now.'

'Much as I'd like to ask you just to leave immediately, I'm not going to do it. We need you here.' Evie turned to face him, forcing herself to look into his eyes and confront some of the painful feelings his arrival had raked up. 'But there's no way on earth that I'd go *anywhere* with you.'

'Sorry to interrupt . . . ' Julia, the practice nurse, tapped on the door and pushed it open without waiting for an invitation. 'It's just that Susie told me about Dr. Joseph arriving, and I had a double appointment first thing who's called in to cancel. So I just wondered if you wanted me to do the surgery tour so you could get on, Evie?'

'That would be fantastic, Julia, thank you so much.' Evie wanted to throw her arms around the other woman. Whether Julia and Susie had overheard anything, she couldn't tell. Either way, the less time she had to spend with David, the better. And now that she had some unexpected free time, the first thing on her list was to contact the agency and see how soon they could arrange another locum to take David's place.

'How's the new locum settling in?' Alasdair's voice was warm, and Evie wanted nothing more than the chance to be with him, face-to-face. But he was spending every moment with Rory — and Bronte too, once she was home from school — and it wasn't something she wanted to encroach upon, as much as she longed to be with him.

'Okay.' She crossed her fingers under the desk as she clutched the phone to her ear with her other hand. It wasn't worth telling him about David; hopefully, he'd be long gone before Alasdair next came into the surgery. She already had the agency on the case.

'You don't exactly sound convinced.'

'He's a competent doctor, but he's about to move to Australia, so I've asked the agency to see if they can find us someone who doesn't have any immediate plans. In case we need a locum for a bit longer. You don't want to rush sending Rory back to school before he's really ready.'

'That sounds like a good idea. And how about you? All that talk of Australia didn't make you want to jump on the next plane?' He was trying to keep his tone light, she could tell, but he didn't quite pull it off.

'Just the opposite, in fact. I told you, I'm here for as long as you need me.' She wanted to say she was there for as long as he *wanted* her, too, but that would just have to wait until she saw him again.

'I really want to see you, but in the evenings the children barely let me move. Rory clings to me as if I'm about to disappear at any moment.' Alasdair sighed. 'And Bronte seems to be a bit jealous of all the attention he's getting. I even caught her putting some red dots on her face with a marker pen!'

'She's so funny, but I suppose it's to be expected that they need that sort of attention from someone they love; they've had so much upheaval in their lives already. I just wish there was something more I could do to help.'

'Just being there is more than enough.' The warmth in his voice enveloped her again, the next best thing to being in his arms. 'I've got to go, but as soon as I get the chance to get away, I'll call you. Okay?'

'Okay, and if there's anything else I can do, just let me know.'

As they ended the call, Evie glanced out of the window, where a single magpie suddenly tapped on the glass, making her jump. *One for sorrow.* She shook off the feeling of foreboding. David would be gone soon, and Rory would be better before they knew it. She could tell Alasdair about her plans to stay on then, and everything would be okay. She was almost sure of it.

10

Evie was doing her best to avoid spending any more time than she had to with David. Thankfully it had been relatively easy for the first couple of days he was at the surgery, since she'd had back-to-back appointments, but the Friday afternoon, which was always left as light as possible so they could catch up on paperwork, was looking much less busy. She had a horrible feeling he'd see that as the perfect excuse for them to talk about going to Australia again. Having got her new mobile number from Susie — who wasn't to know why it shouldn't be given out to their new colleague — he'd been bombarding her with texts about it ever since. Leaving the surgery in the evenings had been an almost covert operation, but thankfully he hadn't gone as far as following her home yet.

He was staying at the Balloch Pass Inn but, if he found out where she lived, he was more than capable of turning up on her doorstep to demand the chance to talk things over again. She'd seen it before and he could be relentless when he wanted something. The agency had promised they'd get someone else sorted for the following week, though, so if she could just make it through the Friday, hopefully he'd get the message and be out of her life for good. She still hadn't told Alasdair about him, their conversations had been filled with Peter and the children, so Evie had wanted to listen rather than talk. David meant nothing to her, so he was hardly worth mentioning anyway.

Normally a home visit call would have added to Evie's stress, but when Susie put Angus McTavish's call through to her just before lunchtime on Friday, it seemed like the perfect excuse to keep out of David's way.

'Dr. Daniels, I'm just ringing because Craig is home from the hospital and I was a bit worried about his medication.' The old man cleared his throat, probably well aware of his reputation for time-wasting in the past. 'I wouldn't normally call you out, only the district nurse isn't due until Monday, and the painkillers he's on don't seem to be agreeing with him.'

'It's not a problem, Mr. McTavish. It'll be good to see him again, under less stressful circumstances this time.' Frankly, even if Craig had just needed two aspirins, Evie would have been happy to drive up to the farm to give them to him. Anything to come back to the surgery and find that David had gone for good. If her blunt text messages back to him hadn't been enough to get the message across, or asking the agency to replace him as soon as possible, then perhaps not even being there to say goodbye on his last day would do the trick. 'I'll be up after lunch. About two o'clock, if that's okay?'

'Aye, that's perfect, Doc.' Angus

sounded much more like his old self. 'You're an angel, saving the day yet again.'

'I'm not sure about that, I'm just happy to help, and see Craig back on his feet as soon as possible.' Putting down the phone, she smiled to herself. If only Angus knew how big a favour he'd just done her, he might even had made himself the hero of the hour.

*   *   *

Alasdair had so wanted to see Evie that he felt like smashing something when he got to the surgery, only to hear from Susie that she'd just gone out on a home visit to the McTavish farm. He only had a couple of hours, before he had to get back to Rory, whose teaching assistant from school had come over to help him catch up on some of the work he'd been missing, now that he was starting to feel better. Alasdair was half tempted to jump in his car and follow Evie up to the farm, but reacting in the way he suspected he might in front of the whole McTavish clan would have looked more than a bit unprofessional. There was no guarantee he'd be able to retain his composure when he saw her again face-to-face. He couldn't fathom quite how much he missed her, when they'd only known each other such a short time. But she'd found this way of getting under his skin and into his heart, even when he'd tried to convince himself that they could just have fun while it lasted.

He should have texted to let her know he was on the way in. The thought of having an hour with Evie had kept him going all day and he'd wanted to surprise her, only now the surprise was on him. He stood in reception for a few minutes after Susie told him that Evie had gone out, reading the posters on the noticeboard but not really taking a word in.

'Ah, so you're the famous Dr. Alasdair James?' A man of a similar age to Alasdair suddenly appeared from the consulting room opposite where he'd been standing. 'I'm David Joseph, the locum.' Looking at his watch the man laughed. 'Well for the next half an hour or so at least.'

'Yes, Dr. Joseph, good to meet you.' Alasdair shook his hand, dredging from the recesses of his brain what Evie had told him. 'I hear you're off to Australia soon and that's why you can't stay with us any longer?'

'Something like that, but call me David, please.' The man narrowed his eyes a bit, as if trying to appraise what Alasdair was saying. 'Sorry, have you got a minute to come into the consulting room? Only there's something I need to hand over to Evie and I think I'll be gone by the time she gets back.'

'Of course.' There was something about the way he said Evie's name that got Alasdair's back up, as if he was far more familiar with her than he ought to have been after a week, drawing out the syllables like they had real meaning to him.

'She has told you who I am, hasn't she?' David turned to look at Alasdair as he closed the consulting room door behind him.

'I thought we'd already established you were the locum.' For a moment Alasdair was wrong-footed, but he didn't miss the smile that crossed David's face.

'We were engaged when we were back in London. I took the job here to try and persuade her to come to Australia with me, I've been offered the chance to set up a new surgery in Sydney and I knew it was somewhere she wanted to go.'

'And what did she say?' The fact that Evie hadn't mentioned her ex-fiancé showing up barely even registered with him. Right now, all he wanted to know was whether she was leaving.

'She said no.' David took something out of the drawer. 'Because of you I suspect. But I know Evie, she might think she loves you and that will be enough for life in a little town like this to fulfil her, but it won't. Because of this.' He dropped the large hard-backed notebook he'd taken out of the drawer onto the table with a thud.

'You don't know anything about me and Evie.'

'But I know *her* and I know all about the promises she made to her mother.' He gestured towards the notebook. 'It's all in there and Australia is just one of the places on a very long list. She might stay for a while, but you'll lose her in the end, just like I did. She's never going to settle until she finishes that list.'

'That's not what she told me about why you two split up.' Alasdair wanted to tell him to get out, to stop saying things he didn't want to hear. He wanted Evie to stay more than anything, but she had to want it too.

'What happened between us doesn't really matter, it was inevitable anyway. Just as it's inevitable she'll leave here too.' David shook his head. 'Look, it's none of my business and all I really wanted was for you to give her this book. She left it behind at my flat when she took off. That's how she went, you know, no warning, she was just gone one day when I got home from work. But if you can live with the prospect of that happening to too at some point, then good luck to you.'

Alasdair took the book from him without saying anything else. David Joseph had landed slap bang in the middle of his daydream and told it like it was. Every day he was growing to love Evie a little bit more and the prospect of her leaving was getting harder to bear. As unwelcome as his words were, David was right. Alasdair couldn't live with the prospect that one day Evie might just up and leave, and he couldn't put the children through that again either. It was going to be hard, but he had to ask Evie to go, while there was still a bit of his heart she wouldn't take with her.

* * *

'I wasn't expecting to see you!' The look of delight on Evie's face when she walked into her consulting room and found Alasdair sitting at her desk made his heart sink. This was going to be more than difficult. He'd been in the process of leaving her a note — and the book that David had given him to pass on — asking her to call him so that they could talk things through. He had to be back at the house soon, but he hadn't wanted to say everything in a note. Even though that would have been much easier.

'I just popped in, whilst Rory's teaching assistant is helping him catch up on some of the school work he's missed, but I've got to be back by four and I need to collect Bronte from the childminder.'

'It's quite something managing family life, isn't it?' Evie smiled. 'But they're more than worth it.'

'They are.' And that was why he had to do what he was about to. Loving Evie and losing her was just going to make things worse for all of them in the end. 'It's been hard with Josh away, but all of this has made me think that we can't just side line what the patients need. This can't just be about us living for the now. I need to know things are going to be stable, for times like this when I might have to be away from the surgery.'

'I've sorted all of that out now with the agency, we've got someone new starting on Monday.'

'I met David.' It was such a short sentence, but it was clear Evie realised the implications before she even spoke.

'And I suppose he told you we already knew each other? I was going to tell you, but it just didn't seem that important to mention whilst you were looking after Rory.'

'Yes, he spoke about that. And a lot more. He told me about the offer for you to go with him to Australia too.' It took all of Alasdair's resolve to say what he did next, but somehow he got the words out. 'I think you should go.'

'With *David*?' Her eyes widened and she looked at him, as if suddenly seeing him for the first time.

'With him, if that's what you want, or just as a colleague, but I meant to Australia. It's an opportunity to live some of those dreams you've talked about and fulfil those promises you made to your mum.' He pushed the book towards her.

'David gave you this?' She lifted the book from the desk, as he nodded his head. 'He must have had it all along when he knew I thought I'd lost it. Whatever he told you about us, we were finished long before mum died. In truth, we just wanted such different things. Her death was just the catalyst that ended things for good.'

'I need someone now who is going to be here — at the surgery — for the long haul.' He didn't want to talk about her and David. It was hard enough getting through this as it was. As Josh had pointed out, just because doing something was the right thing, it didn't necessarily feel like it.

'I was going to tell you when we had a chance to speak properly, but it's never seemed like the right time lately. I'm happy to stay on at the surgery permanently.' Something had shifted in her voice, the warmth leaving it, and she sounded like someone at a job interview trying to convince the panel she would be committed to the role.

'Permanently as in forever?' He couldn't help the surge of hope that accompanied his words, even as she shook her head.

'For a year. At least.' She moved towards him, her voice softening again. 'I know things have been difficult, Alasdair, but I really don't want to leave yet.'

There was that word. *Yet*. Although he was almost certain David hadn't been honest with him about the way he and Evie had ended things, that little word said so much. David was right about that at least. One day, maybe in a year, or two, the time would come when that word would have a devastating impact. Evie would go and maybe Alasdair could live with that, if he didn't let himself love her as completely as he thought he could, he might still get over it one day. But not Rory and Bronte. He couldn't bring Evie deeper into their new lives together, have her share the responsibility of raising Pete and Isabella's precious children, only to walk out on them too one day, when the desire to fulfil the promises to her mother — outlined in that innocent looking notepad — got too much. He could have set fire to the list or hidden it like David clearly had, but it would still have been there, in Evie's heart, waiting for the chance to take her away from him.

'I can't work with a year. Not anymore.' He wanted to tell her about taking over full-time responsibility for the children, but then she might promise to stay for good and maybe she'd even mean it. But emotional blackmail was no basis for a relationship and she'd probably always feel she was forced into making that choice, resenting him for it. No. It was best to just let things go, even though it felt as though it was tearing his heart out.

'So you don't want me to stay?' Her voice was hoarse and he couldn't look at her, in case she saw the lie written on his face and realised her staying was the *only* thing he really wanted, but not on the terms she could offer.

'I think we probably need to contact the agency to see if we can get a locum in who might be interested in a permanent position.' He swallowed hard. 'Of course, I hope you'll stay around until I can get back to work, or at least until the locums are a bit more settled in?' The words he was saying didn't even sound as though they were coming out of his mouth.

'Of course. I'll try to ring them before the offices close today.' There were tears in Evie's eyes, her knuckles turning white as she clutched at the notebook she was holding to her chest.

'I'm sorry things had to end this way, Evie. I just think it will be better for everyone in the long run if we make a clean break now and set the surgery on a new path for the future.' He felt like a politician, trying to sell a line he didn't even believe in.

'If that's what you want.' Her voice was small and he wanted to shout that it was the last thing he wanted, but forcing himself to think of Bronte and Rory he nodded his head and walked to the door of the consulting room, feeling like he'd already lost everything, but knowing the worst was still to come.

★ ★ ★

Evie sat in the chair that Alasdair had just vacated for a full ten minutes without moving. So much for her thinking that her offer to stay on at the surgery for a year would have made him happy. He'd looked horrified, as if he couldn't imagine anything worse. Maybe he'd always banked on her leaving sooner rather than later and what she thought had started to grow between them had only ever been a fling for him. If that was true, then he was a phenomenal actor — he'd certainly had her fooled. Or maybe David had poisoned his mind, but surely he should have believed her rather than a man he'd only just met? She should have told him about David from the start, but would it have made any difference? Something had changed for Alasdair in the last week and made him realise what it was he really wanted. Whatever that was, it clearly wasn't her.

A single tear rolled down Evie's face, gathering momentum as others followed, and fell on the edge of the notepad she was still clutching to her chest. Putting it on the desk, she flicked through some pages, the words blurring behind her tears. She could still make out the places her mother had titled each page with, in her careful handwriting, and some of the pictures she'd cut from magazines and newspapers of the destinations she most wanted to visit.

Then, as she got towards the end, the tears still coming fast, burning her eyes and throat, she came to a page written in purple ink that she was certain she'd never seen before. Taking a tissue from the box on her desk, she tried to stem the tears and clear her vision enough to read the words.

My Dearest Darling Evie
When you read this, I won't be here anymore, but I want you to know I'll still be with you. These last months, spending so much time together, have fulfilled everything I could have wished for. I might not have got to do the things on this list, but talking about them with you and imagining us being there together, laughing about where we'd go and what we'd see, has got me through the hardest time in my life with so much joy.

I hope you get to see the world and visit all the places on this list, but most of all I want you to have someone to share that with. Someone who shares and supports <u>your</u> dreams — just as you have mine for the past few months — rather than someone who foists theirs on you.

I hope you see the world together with adventure and laughter, but most of all love. Even if you never leave London in the end, if true love finds you there, I'll be looking down, knowing that the very most important thing on my wish list has come true.

All my love, my best girl.

Mum xxxx

By the time Evie had finished reading the note from her mother, it was as if there were no tears left, her body shaking with emotion instead. All her mother had ever truly wanted was for Evie to find someone who could love her in the way her mum thought she deserved. Asking Evie to promise to see the world had been about opening her eyes up to see David as he really was, although he'd done that for himself in the end. If only Evie had read through the notebook straight away after her mother died, before it disappeared, maybe things with Alasdair would have been so different. Or maybe she was just fooling herself again. He didn't want her, he'd made that much clear, so he couldn't be the man her mother wanted for her, even though Evie had wanted him to be more than she dared admit.

Picking up her phone, she scrolled down to the number of the locum agency. Maybe they'd have someone looking for a permanent position who'd be ready to start next week. After all, she deserved a bit of luck, didn't she? A day or two's handover and she could leave Balloch Pass behind, but now she had no idea where she wanted to go and only more fractures on her already broken heart to show for the time she'd spent there. Forgetting all about Alasdair James was her new priority, but there was no fooling herself this time — it was going to be anything but easy.

11

The agency had managed to identify a
locum from their staffing bank who
might be willing to consider a switch to
a permanent role if he found the work
in Balloch Pass to his liking. He'd
started work on the Monday, alongside
the other locum that Evie had arranged
to replace David. Having successfully
managed to derail her relationship with
Alasdair, David had left town on the
Friday without a backward glance.
She'd been right, it had always been
about winning one way or another for
him, and getting one up on Evie had
obviously been all he needed to repair
his wounded ego. If the pain of falling
for Alasdair had any upside, it was
knowing now one hundred percent that
she'd been right to leave David and her
life in London behind.

Evie had already packaged up her few

meagre boxes of belongings at the cottage and she'd taken to carrying her mum's notebook with her everywhere, determined not to lose sight of it again. Julia and Susie had stepped up to the challenge of having two new locums at the surgery and so she wouldn't need to stick around for much longer to complete the handover. Soon they'd be nothing left to keep her in Balloch Pass, least of all Alasdair. He'd made that abundantly clear and, even though she felt as if he'd reached in and pulled her heart right out of her chest when he'd asked her to go, at least he'd been honest. Rory was back at school, but only for half days, until he felt fully fit, and Josh still wasn't back, so Alasdair had decided to take another week or two off work. At least that meant she wasn't having to deal with him being at work for her last few days.

She'd driven out to say her goodbyes to the McTavish family straight after work on the Wednesday afternoon and to check on Craig one final time. It was already dark by the time she made her way back down into the village and she had to brake quite sharply when she saw a car stopped almost diagonally across the normally quiet road, its hazard lights flashing.

Trying not to think about every horror film she'd ever seen, Evie had to decide whether to get out of the car or not. Just as she was contemplating what to do, another vehicle pulled in behind her, its headlights dazzling in her rear view mirror. Shivering, she suddenly felt very alone. What it if was some sort of set up and she was out here now, stranded between two cars in the dark, in the middle of nowhere? She'd heard about doctors being followed before and car-jacked for their medical supplies. She let out a scream as someone knocked on the window of her car.

'Evie, what an earth's going on?' Alasdair was looking at her through the side window of the car and for a moment she wasn't sure whether to be relieved or not. She'd been hoping that she might be able to leave town without seeing him again, as if that might somehow make it easier.

'I don't know, I just got here and the car in front was blocking the road. I wasn't sure . . . ' She didn't finish the sentence, it suddenly seemed silly to assume that something like that would happen somewhere as quiet as Balloch Pass. It was hardly the mean streets of the big city.

'You stay here and I'll go and a have a look.' Alasdair might have been trying to protect her, but she was already opening her door as he spoke.

As they approached the car, the door swung open and a young man in his mid-twenties jumped out, his eyes wide with panic. Looking past him towards the passenger seat, it was obvious to see why. There was a heavily pregnant woman, clearly in agony and every bit as terrified as the driver.

'Thank goodness.' The man's face was drained of all colour. 'We've got a flat tyre and I can't seem to get the wheel off, the spanner kept slipping off. I don't think it's even the right one.' He was close to tears and speaking so quickly it was difficult to make out what he was saying.

'My mobile phone has gone dead as well.' He gestured towards the useless phone, which he'd thrown on the seat at the back of the car. 'I didn't know what to do. April thinks the baby's coming and I . . . ' He trailed off and looked at Alasdair and Evie as if they were his only hope.

'It's okay. We're both doctors.' Alasdair laughed, as the younger man reached out and grabbed him round the neck in a sort of awkward hug.

'I thought we were having the worst luck in the world, but I've never been so glad to see a doctor in my life.'

'What we really need to do is take a look at April, see how urgent the situation is and phone through for ambulance.' Alasdair passed his mobile to the young man. 'I'm Alasdair and this is Evie.'

'Sean.' The young man looked over at the passenger seat as he spoke. 'And you already know my wife's name.'

'Okay, Sean, if you can move aside for a moment, so Evie and I can take a look at April?' Alasdair looked at Evie as she nodded. They didn't need to exchange words, they'd just had a sort of symmetry to be able to work together, almost seamlessly, since the day she'd first seen him at the railway crossing.

Evie went around to the other side of the car and opened April's door, her face was grey with pain and she was grimacing with the sensation of each contraction, which seemed to be gripping her body almost constantly. 'Okay, April, you're doing fine. We're here to help now.'

'Use my phone to call for an ambulance.' Alasdair's voice was calm as he spoke to Sean and, despite everything, there was no-one Evie would rather have been there with. 'We'll need to get April to the hospital as soon as possible.'

It was obvious from the frequency of the contractions that the baby could arrive before the ambulance, but neither Evie or Alasdair said it out loud. The couple were already terrified and all Evie could hope was that, if there were any complications, the two of them would be able to cope with it.

'How are you doing sweetheart?' Alasdair had moved to kneel on the driver's seat, his voice gentle and reassuring, and April managed to turn her head and look at him.

'I've been better.' The young woman gripped the dashboard in front of her as another contraction came. 'Where's Sean? He promised not to leave me.' The words came out in short rasps as the contraction finally began to subside.

'He's just using Alasdair's mobile to phone for an ambulance.' Not sure whether April had even heard her, Evie put a hand over hers. 'I'm Evie and this is Alasdair, we're both doctors and we want to take a look at you to see if there's anything we can do to help before the ambulance arrives.'

'I think we should push the seat back and see if we can get April to lie back in a more comfortable position.' Evie looked at Alasdair as he spoke and nodded in response. If April was about to give birth they'd need as much room as possible to try and help the baby out. Ideally it would have been better to move April on to the back seat of the car, but at this stage it would probably be too traumatic.

'I'll support April's back while you lower the car seat.' Alasdair leant further forward and placed an arm behind April, pulling her closer towards him, whilst Evie lowered the back of the seat as much as she could, until the headrest was only an inch or so above the back seat, pushing it back as far as it would go to make some room in the footwell before Alasdair gently lowered April down.

'The ambulance is on its way.' Sean wrenched open the back door of the car as he spoke and slid in behind the driver's seat, so that he was able to reach over and hold April's hand without getting in the way.

'That's great.' Evie turned towards him. 'Is this April's first baby?' When Sean nodded, she exchanged a quick glance with Alasdair, as the pace of her own breathing involuntarily quickened. 'How long has she been in labour?' First babies usually took a bit longer to arrive, but Evie had a horrible feeling April's firstborn wasn't the sort to wait around.

'About two hours.' Sean glanced at his watch has he spoke. 'We thought we'd have hours to get to the hospital, so she had a bath and everything first.'

'We need to take your trousers off, so that we can see if the baby's on its way.' Alasdair spoke softly to April, who just nodded in response, the labour pains obviously outweighing any other feelings she might have about being examined by two strangers in the most unconventional of places to give birth.

Evie and Alasdair moved quickly, as if delivering a baby in a car at the side of the road was something they did every day.

'It's almost time.' Evie looked up at Alasdair as she spoke. She could see the top of the head.

'Your baby's nearly here.' Alasdair leant towards April. 'You're doing brilliantly, sweetheart, and you can start to push in a minute or two. I just need to get a few things out of my car that you and the baby might need, but Evie's with you.'

'Sean, we need to slide that blanket under April's back and bottom if we can. It will make it easier for the baby to be born if there are a couple of inches between April and the surface of the seat.' Evie gestured towards a tartan blanket that lay across the parcel shelf at the back of the car. Sean's eyes were still wide with panic, but he did as he was told.

'Thanks. Now if you can try and raise April up slightly so that I can slide the blanket underneath her.' Evie folded the blanket in four and managed to ease it onto the seat, as April screamed out in pain.

'I want to push!' The young woman was suddenly insistent, her face screwed up.

'Just a few more minutes April, I promise.' Evie prayed she sounded calmer than she felt. 'I'm going to try to make things a bit easier for you now.' April gripped the handbrake as she struggled to control the pain and Evie helped her to move her legs into a more comfortable position.

Alasdair suddenly appeared at Evie's side and she was more relieved than ever at whatever twist of fate had meant they were both here for this. He smiled at her for a moment as if they'd never had that conversation about her leaving. Then he turned towards the terrified father-to-be.

'Do you know if you're expecting a boy or a girl?'

'We wanted a surprise.' Sean tried to

laugh, but it cracked a bit. 'I don't think either of us realised quite how much of a surprise it was going to be.'

'I think we're ready.' Evie glanced at Alasdair again, before turning towards April. 'I want you to put your chin on your chest and give this baby a really big push out into the world.'

As April began to push, Alasdair counted out loud, the young woman raising herself slightly off the seat as she gave every ounce of her energy she had. Exhausted, she collapsed back on to the seat.

'You're doing wonderfully sweetheart.' He looked down towards where Evie was crouching and she nodded her head again, it was definitely time. 'Just a few more good pushes like that and you'll be able to meet your baby.'

'I can't do it anymore, I'm too tired.'

'Of course you can darling.' Sean stroked her hair, trying to reassure her.

'You can keep your mouth shut!' April turned her head sharply towards him, but at least her anger had given her a renewed sense of energy. 'Okay, I'm ready to push now.' Lowering her chin on to her chest, she pushed as Alasdair counted again.

'Okay, keep going.' Evie could hardly keep the excitement out of her voice. 'The baby's coming!' Suddenly she could see the back of the baby's head as is emerged into the world. 'Stop pushing for a minute, April.' Supporting the baby's head, Evie turned it slightly to make sure it could be delivered safely.

Alasdair was at her side and they were working as a team again without the need to speak and it didn't seem possible that this was the last time they would. Evie pushed that thought to the back of her head and looked up at April again. This was one of life's miracles and at that moment all that mattered was this young family.

'Okay, that's great. I need you to push just once more April.'

With one final effort, the baby finally arrived, straight into Evie's waiting hands. Between them, she and Alasdair moved swiftly to check the baby over, and then then there was the most glorious sound Evie thought she'd ever heard, as April and Sean's baby gave its first hearty cry.

Lying the baby on its mother's chest, Evie took the blankets that Alasdair passed her and covered the two of them up. The most important thing now was that they kept warm until the ambulance arrived.

'Is it a boy or a girl?' Sean asked the question suddenly, tears streaming down his face as he looked from Evie to Alasdair and back again.

'Oh, my goodness, I'm sorry. In all the excitement I forgot to say.' Evie couldn't hold back the smile that was tugging at the corners of her mouth any longer 'Congratulations. You've got a little boy.'

* * *

'What were you doing all the way out here?' Alasdair turned to look at Evie as the ambulance carrying the new little family of three sped away into the darkness. One of the paramedics had helped Alasdair push the couple's car into a passing place, so it wouldn't block the road until a recovery truck could pick it up, so there was nothing stopping them heading their separate ways now, but he couldn't help thinking that something must have put them together on this same road at the same time.

'I went to say goodbye to the McTavish family and check on Craig one last time before I leave, he's doing really well. And then I just felt like driving for a bit before I went back to the cottage.' She didn't seem quite able to look him in the face as she spoke and he could understand why. He might have been wanting to protect Rory and Bronte, but he'd hurt Evie in the process and that was something he had to put right. He couldn't let her leave without knowing the real reason he'd asked her to go. 'What about you? I thought you'd be with the children.'

'Josh is back but he's whipped the children up into a frenzy of excitement, but failed to mention he'll be going away again soon.' Alasdair shook his head. 'I just had to get out and drive for a bit too, grab an hour or so to clear my head.'

'I don't suppose this is quite what you envisaged?' She managed a half smile and he wanted to hold her in his arms and tell her what an idiot he'd been and that finding her on the road had felt like a sign from somewhere, as crazy as that sounded. But she needed a rational explanation, it was the least she deserved.

'Not quite, but I just needed some time to think, to process everything that's happening.'

'Can Josh keep doing this, just going away I mean?' Evie shivered as they stood in the road in front of her car, the headlights illuminating the darkness. 'They're going to need someone who can put them first.'

'He can't do that anymore, the pull to go back to work is just too strong for him.' If Alasdair had been planning to dress it up for her, then she'd opened the door to the plain truth. 'When Pete and Isabella asked me to become the children's guardian we talked about the reasons why he couldn't just leave it to Josh and neither of them wanted the children moved to Isabella's family in Italy. It was just one of those pie-in-the-sky conversations at the time, about something that was never actually going to happen. But all the same, I promised Pete that if Josh couldn't be there for the children because of his work, I'd bring them up in Balloch Pass, in the same house they've always lived in. That's why I'm tied here, why I can't ever make plans to leave this place. Not even for you.'

'Why didn't you tell me?' Evie turned to face him now, really looking at him for the first time. 'I would have understood.'

'I didn't want you to make promises

about staying here — for me or the children — that you'd come to resent.' Alasdair took her hand and she didn't snatch it away. 'I could risk loving you and losing you, but I can't let Bronte and Rory risk that. They've lost far too much already.'

'I know, but I just wished you'd told me, trusted me instead of David.' The hurt that he'd caused was naked in her eyes and he hated himself for it. She was right, he should have known Evie would never do anything to hurt the children. If he'd been honest with her, they'd have found a way to make it work for all of them. He might have left it too late, but he had to ask.

'I'm sorry, I just didn't know how to tell you without making the children some sort of lever to make you stay. This was never the life I envisaged for myself, taking on two children and becoming a dad almost overnight. But I love those kids with all my heart and all I want to do now is to make things as right for them as I can.' He traced a line down the side of her face with such tenderness that she couldn't doubt his feelings. 'But even though I wanted you in my life just as much, I couldn't ask you to do that, you've got your own dreams to pursue and I can't ask you to put them to one side just for me.'

'Alasdair James, you're an idiot. The only dreams I have now are about you and me and finding a way to hold onto this amazing thing we've found.' She was smiling, silencing his response by gently pressing her lips against his, before pulling away from him again. 'I love you and I think in a roundabout way you're trying to tell me you love me too.'

'I do love you, probably from the first moment I saw you. I know I've been an idiot and I'm sorry.'

'We'll talk about that again later.' She laughed, as he raised his eyebrows in response. 'But someone once told me the most important thing in life is not just to follow your dreams, but to find someone who shares them with you.

And I think we've found that.'

'I know I have.' Pulling Evie into his arms at last, he kissed her. Not even stopping when the headlights of her car suddenly went off, plunging the road into darkness. Despite the lack of light, he'd never been able to see more clearly in his life.

★   ★   ★

'It's okay. You can just drop me off by the pub and I'll walk back up to the cottage.' Evie could hardly believe she'd left her headlights on and drained the car battery, especially when she knew Alasdair needed to get back to the children and try to convince Josh that putting off telling them that he was definitely leaving — now he'd formally been offered a job in the Philippines — was just prolonging the agony.

'I know it's a lot to ask, but will you come back to the house with me?' Alasdair looked at her for a moment before turning back towards the road. 'I nearly lost you once and the thought of you being there to help the children cope with hearing about Josh leaving, makes me think they'll handle it much better. I know that's not really fair on you, though.'

'We're in this together. *All* of it.' Evie could barely get her head around how much her life had changed in the last hour or so. They'd brought a new life into the world together and they were about to wave Josh off to the other side of the world. Somewhere along the line they'd made a pact to be in it for the long haul too, taking care of Rory and Bronte. It was as if she'd woken up and found herself in someone else's life, but it was what she wanted. Her mother had been right, sharing even the tiniest part of the world with someone was more important than seeing the whole thing on your own. When she'd kissed Alasdair and the headlights had gone out on her car, it had felt more like a sign from her mother than the result of a flat battery. She couldn't drive off anymore because she didn't need to. And she didn't want to either. Alasdair had even said that he didn't want to stand in the way of her dreams. If that wasn't a sign then she wasn't sure what was. It had been easy in the end, looking into his eyes and knowing that he meant every word; that he loved her. It was all she'd needed to hear to make her want to stay forever.

'Are you ready?' He turned to look at her again as they pulled up outside the house and for the first time she was scared. Not because of the promise she'd made to be with Alasdair, but of what they'd find behind the innocent-looking front door. The children had already lost both their parents and now their uncle was moving on too. Could she and Alasdair really give them what they needed?

'What do you want me to do when we go inside?' It felt as though they needed to rehearse it, so they could find some way of helping the children cope.

'If you can just have a chat with the

kids, whilst I have a word with Josh, that would be great. I know they're going to be excited to see you.' Alasdair sighed. 'Josh keeps insisting that he should wait until the day before he flies out to the Philippines before he tells them, so they can enjoy their last few days together before he goes. But I think he's trying to protect himself as much as he is them, so he doesn't have to deal with their emotions for any longer than he has to.'

'I suppose I can see his point, but we're the ones who are going to be left helping them through this latest change and if they realise we knew long before they did, they might start to resent it.'

'Even if it doesn't feel like it to you.' He cupped one hand on the side of her face. 'I want you to know how much it means to me that you're here, what a difference it's making. Just being able to talk to you is like a weight lifting off me.'

'I love you.' She put her hand over his, locking the moment into her memory. The start of their new life together.

'I love you too.' Alasdair withdrew his hand. 'I wish it didn't have to be like this, I should be making things up to you for being such an idiot and instead I'm dragging you into all of this.'

'No you're not. We're going to get through this, together. The rest of it can wait, we've got no limit on the time we can spend together now.' Following him into the house seconds later, she held her breath, hoping she could be enough for him and the children when it mattered the most.

★   ★   ★

'I've missed you!' Bronte almost knocked Evie sideways as she ran down the corridor from the kitchen. 'Uncle Alasdair said you'd been busy at work, but I wanted to show you the friendship bracelets I've been making, because I've got some for you.' The little girl shook her wrist vigorously and about ten plastic bracelets jangled together as she did so.

'I've missed you too, darling.' Evie returned her hug as Bronte wrapped her arms around her neck, squeezing as tightly as her little arms would let her.

'Uncle Alasdair wouldn't wear a bracelet, he said they get in the way when he's working with patients.' Bronte wrinkled her nose. 'But it's probably because he thinks friendship bracelets are only for girls.'

'I'm sure that's not true.'

'Yes it is, even Rory said so!'

Evie fought the urge to smile, despite the situation. Bronte was still her old self, full of almost-six-year-old opinion and no-one could persuade her she was wrong.

'Where is Rory?' Evie looked around the kitchen as she and Bronte finally make it back to the other end of the corridor, the little girl still clamped to her like a limpet. Alasdair had already disappeared to talk to Josh.

'He's in his room, I expect. Crying again.'

'Why is he crying?' Evie dug her fingernails into the palm of her hand, not sure if she wanted to hear the answer. Maybe Bronte knew more than she was letting on about Josh leaving.

'Because we aren't going on holiday!' Bronte put her hands on her hips. 'He said Josh is too busy to take us on holiday this year and it's not fair, but I told him he was the one who wasn't being fair when Uncle Josh has to go to work sometimes to pay for stuff. He said I was stupid and I told Uncle Josh on him and then he started to cry and he won't come out of his room.'

'Poor Rory, do you think we should go upstairs and speak to him?' Evie didn't want to leave Bronte on her own downstairs, but she was worried that Rory might blurt out the truth about Josh, before their uncle had the chance to tell them in his own words. Still, it was a risk she was going to have to take, there was no way she could leave Rory up there alone when he'd clearly already guessed what was about to happen.

'How are my two favourite girls doing?' She hadn't noticed Alasdair walk back through to the kitchen until she heard his voice.

'We were just about to go up to speak to Rory, he's been very upset about his uncle not being able to take him on holiday.' Evie was doing her best to keep her voice even, whilst Bronte was still amusing herself playing with the bracelets on her wrist.

'I've spoken to Josh and he's just printing out some pictures.' Alasdair hesitated for a moment as he ruffled Bronte's hair. 'To help him explain things to everyone.'

'I think that's probably a good idea. Do you still want me to come up to Rory's room with you?'

'Please.' As he spoke, Alasdair hoisted Bronte on to his back. 'This is what my dad used to call a fireman's lift. He took me upstairs to bed like this every night until I got too big to carry.'

'I'm not going to bed yet, Uncle Alasdair.'

'I know, angel, but Evie and I want to have a little chat with you and Rory and so we're going to go up and find him.'

'Okay. If we *have* to.'

Evie hung back behind Alasdair as he got Bronte to lean over his shoulder and knock on her brother's bedroom door.

'Go away.'

'It's Uncle Alasdair and I've got Evie with me.'

'Come in then.' Rory turned over on his bed, as they walked into the room, looking at them briefly and then fixing his eyes firmly on the ceiling. 'You didn't say you had *Bronte-the-pain* with you too.'

'Don't talk like that, Rory, you two need to be nice to each other.' Alasdair took Bronte off his back and sat her on the end of bed, moving to stand next to Evie.

'What, because Uncle Josh is going to leave us for good now too, just like mum and dad did? So I've got to be nice to *her*?'

'Stop saying things about Uncle Josh leaving. I hate you!' Bronte stuck out her tongue.

'Not half as much as I hate you. It's probably your fault he's going anyway, he probably hates you too!'

'Stop saying that, both of you.' Alasdair caught hold of Bronte as she launched herself towards her brother.

'It's true, I don't want to be left on my own with her!' As Rory's voice shook with far more emotion than any eight-year-old should have to deal with, Evie moved towards the side of the bed and sat down on the edge of it. She looked up at Alasdair raising a questioning eyebrow and, when he nodded, she turned back towards Rory.

'Do you understand what's happening with your Uncle Josh?'

'He's just sulking 'cos of the holiday!' Bronte was wriggling in Alasdair's arms, still wanting to get free and take out all her pent-up emotion on her brother.

'It's got nothing to do with that,

stupid!' Rory's face twisted as he spoke, taking the situation out of their hands. 'It's because Uncle Josh has got a new job a long way away. I saw a letter he'd left in the kitchen. I didn't understand all of it, but I know he's leaving us!'

'He is not!' Bronte was crying now as well, her arms and legs flailing as Alasdair struggled to hold on to her.

Evie pulled Rory towards her and he buried his head in her shoulder, his little body shaking.

'Oh darling, I know this is hard, but Uncle Josh is not going to go away for ever. The reason he's leaving has got nothing to do with either of you, he loves you both so much. He'll be back for visits whenever he can and maybe he'll even come back for good eventually.'

'But you can't promise that, can you?' Rory pulled away and looked up at her, another bit of her heart breaking as she shook her head.

'But Uncle Josh can't go.' Bronte was still fighting in Alasdair's arms and Evie looked up at him, their eyes meeting for

279

the briefest of moments. 'Who's going to look after us? I don't want to go and live with Auntie Maria in *It-Lee*.' Five-year-olds had an amazing way of boiling things down to the basics, even in the most difficult situations and Bronte was no exception.

'You won't have to, darling. You can stay right here, in your house, at your old school and I'll look after you, with Evie.'

'But what if you decide to leave us too?' Bronte was sobbing now, struggling to get the words out properly.

'We'll never do that, sweetheart, that's one thing I can promise.' Alasdair stroked her hair. 'In fact, Evie and I can't believe how lucky we are getting to be the ones who look after you and Rory. Forever.'

'Uncle Josh is leaving soon, isn't he?' Rory looked up at Evie again and she forced herself to nod. Despite Alasdair's reassurances, it had been as hard for the children to hear that someone else they loved was leaving as she'd feared it might be. They were too young to really understand why Josh felt he had to go. All the medical training in the world couldn't make some things right and sometimes being there was all you could do.

12

Josh stayed on with the children for another four days and took them up to the lodge with him so they'd have a last adventure together before he left. Bronte made him a bracelet to wear with his favourite coloured beads and there'd been tears in his eyes when she'd put it on his wrist. Alasdair had driven Josh to the airport, whilst Evie had stayed at home snuggled up under a blanket on the sofa with the children, in front of a Disney movie none of them were really watching.

The children had done that incredible thing that kids often did, of putting the adults around them to shame with and after the initial upset they'd dealt with it really well. All the same Alasdair had decided they needed him around full-time for the foreseeable future, to make sure they realised how stable their home-life now was. Evie was going into the surgery most days to check on things, but Susie and Julia were doing a great job in their absence, supporting the locums and making sure the surgery kept running.

Alasdair wasn't naïve enough to think everything was back to normal and that the children were completely unaffected, but he so glad they seemed able to tell him and Evie what it was they wanted. They were a team now, the four of them, and they involved the children as much as they could in every decision they made. They'd even chosen the kitten that Alasdair had promised them on that trip to the zoo and agreed that a puppy could follow, once Buttons was old enough to put it in its place. Bronte had admitted she was glad that her Uncle Josh had gone, even though she missed him, because she liked being in a family of four again. Rory had nodded, but he was far less vocal than his sister and it sometimes worried Alasdair that there was more under the surface with him. Life had changed beyond all recognition and so quickly, but despite all of that somehow they fitted together, like it was meant to be.

The days since Josh had left had sealed his feelings for Evie, too, and he couldn't help smiling, remembering his best friend telling him he'd know when he found the love of his life, just as Pete had done with Isabella. He'd been right, that it would be obvious when the time came, and Alasdair couldn't have been more certain it was Evie if it had been written in mile-high letters across the sky. They all needed something to look forward to and he'd promised himself the children would be just as involved when he proposed. He wanted to wait a while, despite having found the perfect ring, because it just didn't seem to be the right time yet. He'd had to hide it where no-one would think to look, especially as Bronte was a bit like a magpie, picking up anything shiny she found and hiding it in her room. But when the moment came, Rory and

Bronte would be part of the proposal too. They were a family now.

They all had their down days, but even in the midst of it all there was a lot of laughter in the house and Alasdair had been so proud of the comfortable way the children spoke about their parents, which seemed to make it easier for them to cope, keeping them alive in their memory. So when he went up to Rory's room one lunchtime and found him gone, a post-it note stuck to his iPad, saying he'd gone to see his parents, it was as if someone had kicked Alasdair's legs out from under him.

'Evie, it's me. I've just been up to Rory's room to call him down for lunch and he's gone.' Thankfully the call went straight through to her mobile. She was the only other person who'd understand how terrified he felt at that moment.

'Are you sure he's not somewhere else in the house?' She was trying to keep calm, but he didn't miss the way her voice had risen.

'He's left a note, saying he's gone to be with his mum and dad. I think he must mean where their ashes were scattered.'

'Up near the lodge?'

'That's all I can think of.' Alasdair shuddered at the thought. There was no way Rory could make it all the way up to the track to get to the lodge, he'd take the short route he'd sometimes walked with Josh and his dad before that. But it meant crossing the river and, at this time of year, after the recent heavy rain, it was high in places, and flowing much more quickly than it would be safe to cross.

'Has he packed an inhaler?'

'I don't know, I hadn't even thought about that.'

'I'll call Millie's mum and ask her if Bronte can stay on there a bit longer, while we look for him.' Evie had been due to pick her up from her best friend's house after she finished the monthly Saturday morning surgery. They'd both got used to putting the children first. And whilst they hadn't decided yet on any long-term plans for managing their new role as parents, alongside their jobs, it had been something else they'd worked at together, as seamlessly as they had before. Now it was almost as if she was able to read his mind. 'Do you think we should call the police?'

'Not yet.' Alasdair didn't want to think about what might happen if they didn't get to Rory before he crossed the river, but no-one knew the route up to the lodge better than him, so the police would be a long way behind them, even if they called them now. 'I'll meet you on the road, where the footpath sign leads up to Coille Water.'

'I'm less than five minutes away.' Evie sound breathless already. 'He is going to be okay isn't he?'

'He'll be fine.' Disconnecting the call, Alasdair grabbed his keys, praying he was right.

* * *

Evie left her car with two wheels on the grass bank, as close to the footpath as she could park it. Racing towards the sign, at the same time as she spotted Alasdair running down the hill to meet her.

'He'll have headed up to Folder's Crossing, it's the narrowest part of the river at this end of the forest, but the water's still high and fast at this time of year.'

'Is there a bridge?' Evie shivered at the thought of Rory up there alone.

'Just a series of stones, but they'll be at least partially covered by the height of the water at this time of year.'

'How long does it take to get up there?' Evie spoke as she followed Alasdair onto the footpath, neither of them wanting to waste a moment.

'Not more than ten minutes from here, but I checked and I think Rory took the big camping rucksack with him that Peter always used when they went up there for the weekend. If he's got that loaded with stuff, it might take him a bit longer.' He turned to look at her for a moment, his face seeming to drain of colour. 'At least that's what I'm hoping.'

The leaves crunched underfoot as they half ran, half walked up the hill into the woods to Folder's Cross, neither of them speaking much. Evie tried to push the unwanted thoughts out of her head. What if they didn't find him in time? Or if they did find him and he was seriously hurt? Falling in love with Alasdair had been a huge surprise by itself. But the way her love for Bronte and Rory had grown so quickly too, took her breath away. She couldn't imagine life without any one of them. And she didn't want to.

'He's up ahead, I can see him.' Alasdair pointed towards the bank of the river and Evie could just see Rory's white-blond hair above the top of it.

'Is he in the water?'

'I don't know. Rory, stop!' Alasdair shouted so loudly a couple of birds rose up from the tree beside them.

'I don't think he can hear us.' Evie was breathless, they were both running full-pelt now, but nothing could have stopped her. They had to get to him.

'Oh no, he's in the river,' Alasdair spoke as they got closer. Rory was in the water, still clinging to the rucksack that seemed to be wedged sideways, partially submerged in front of him.

'Help! I've slipped and my bag's stuck, but it keeps moving and I don't know if I can hold on.'

'I'm going in to get him.' Alasdair was already starting to take his jacket off.

'No, let me. If you fall too and the current takes you further downstream, there's no way I'll be able to pull the two of you out, but if you hold onto my ankles, I should be able to lie on my stomach to reach him and pull him back across.'

'Evie, you can't . . . '

'There isn't time for an argument.' She didn't want to state the obvious. If the current dislodged the rucksack it would take Rory with it and if he hit his head on the rocks, anything could happen to him. 'I'm coming to get you, darling.'

Evie got as close to the edge of the river bank as she could without falling in. Alasdair took hold of both her ankles and she slithered into the water, the rocks that made Folder's Crossing passable in the summer just below her. Reaching out her hands as far as she could, she managed to grab Rory under his arms.

'I don't want to let go of the rucksack.' He looked at her, his eyes huge in the pallor of his face.

'I know darling, but you've got to trust me. I've got you and Alasdair's got us both.'

'It's not just that, there's something in there. A book I made for Mum and Dad.'

'Okay, Rory, let me get you to Alasdair first and I promise we'll try and come back for it.'

Rory hesitated for a moment and

then released his grip on the bag. He felt a lot heavier than she'd imagined, but his clothes were soaked and the current was doing its best to pull them apart. But there was no way she was letting that happen.

'I'm slipping.' Rory almost seemed to be fighting her, his arms and legs flailing in panic, as she fought just as hard to hold onto him, her fingers gripping so tightly to the clothes he was wearing that they hurt. But at that moment she realised she'd have died for him. It was what being a parent was.

'I promise I won't let you go.' As she spoke, Alasdair was pulling them back towards him and for a second her grip on Rory slipped, as the water flow pulled them in different directions. The little boy shot her a terrified look as Evie grabbed another handful of his coat, clenching her hands tighter still; determined to keep her promise. And, just when it felt it might never end, Alasdair pulled them both back onto the bank and into his arms.

'I'll never ask for anything again, knowing you're both safe.' Alasdair kissed the top of her head, holding on to her as if he might never let her go, Rory clamped to him on the other side. As the little boy shivered, Alasdair took his discarded jacket and wrapped it around Rory, as Evie pulled him onto her lap. 'Is your breathing okay? Do you need your inhaler?'

'No, I'm fine, but my bag! It's got something really important in it.' Suddenly Rory gave a shout as the current finally dislodged the rucksack. It took all of Evie's strength to hold on to him, he was so desperate to get the bag back. Alasdair leapt to his feet and ran down the river bank, hitting the water with a splash.

'Alasdair!' She barely had time to shout his name, panic clawing at her throat again as he went out of view for a moment, but seconds later he was scrabbling up the bank towards them.

'You better not just have cheese and pickle sandwiches in here, Rory.'

Alasdair handed over the bag.

'I made this for Mum and Dad, it's like Evie's book for her mum.' He pulled out a notebook from the rucksack. It was a professional camping bag, designed to withstand any weather, so despite its plunge in the river the contents were still dry.

'Can I have a look?' Evie took the book from him. He'd stuck photographs, postcards and some of his own drawings in there, a few of the place names were misspelt, but it was his own version of the list Evie had made with her mother.

'It's all the places Mum and Dad said they'd take me before they died. Mum always said that one day we'd go to Africa and see the elephants in the wild. And Dad promised to take me to swim with dolphins. When he first moved in, Uncle Josh said we might be able to go and see the dolphins with him instead.' Rory shook his head. 'Bronte thought I was upset about not going on holiday but it wasn't that, it was because we'd never get to see all those places with Mum and Dad. That's why I wanted Josh to take me so much, so I could see them for Mum and Dad.'

'Oh darling, I know it's not fair.' Evie had barely started speaking before Rory shook his head.

'I *was* really sad, but then I started thinking about your book.' He looked down at his soaking wet shoes for a second and then up at Evie again. 'Remember when we were at the zoo and I told you about my 'one day' box? I wanted to turn it into a book like you've got, so I could take it with me everywhere. Then when I finally get to go to these places, I can tell mum and dad all about them when I come back here. That's why I wanted to come to the lodge today, to tell them both what I was planning to do.'

'That's a great idea.' Alasdair took Evie's hand in his, another unspoken message passing between them. 'And maybe the four of us — you, me, Bronte and Evie — can work our way through both lists together. Just promise me one thing?'

'What?'

'That you won't pull a stunt like this again? We're a family now and if one of us is going on an adventure — at the lodge or anywhere else for that matter — then *all* of us are.'

'I promise, but only if you promise me something too.' Rory grinned mischievously and Evie felt Alasdair's grip on her hand tighten.

'Okay.'

'You've got to tell me what this is for?' Rory pulled a ring box out of the pocket of the jacket Alasdair had given him.

'If I tell you, you can't tell Bronte that you knew first and when we do this all over again, you have to act surprised, alright?' Alasdair raised his eyebrows and Rory nodded with all the seriousness an eight year old could muster. Evie caught her breath, as Alasdair reached over and took the box out of the little boy's hands.

'This is not quite how I'd planned to do this, but Rory's caught me out and suddenly now seems as good at time as any. I got the ring last week and put it in the pocket of a jacket I don't wear anymore, so no-one would find it. When I was running out of the house this afternoon, I just grabbed the first jacket I could find, but now it feels like it was meant to be.' Turning Evie to face him, he knelt down beside her. 'Evie Daniels, I love you. More than I ever thought possible. And I know you love me, more than I thought I'd ever deserve to be loved. I want us to build a forever in Balloch Pass and for the four of us to see the world together, which Rory here seems to have an excellent plan for. I thought maybe we could start with a honeymoon, somewhere you and the kids could both cross off places from your wish lists, maybe even somewhere that has dolphins? Will you marry me, Evie?'

'A million times, yes.' She moved towards him, as he slipped the ring on her finger, sure that somewhere her mother was looking down and smiling as she finally got the thing she'd wanted most for her daughter. As Alasdair took her into his arms and kissed her, it was pretty much the perfect moment.

'Yuck, Uncle Alasdair, don't do that!' Rory registered his disapproval and she pulled away from Alasdair laughing, as her brand new fiancé asked one more question.

'Are you sure this is what you want?'

'Absolutely. I've never been more certain of anything.' Taking his hand, she put her other arm around Rory. It might not have been the type of adventure she'd expected, but life was never going to be dull with the three people she loved most in her life and, as far as she was concerned, that was the best adventure anyone could wish for.